Quinn's Quest

Hope you enjoy Quinn's journey; Gloria O'Shields

Gloria O'Shields

iUniverse, Inc.
New York   Bloomington

Quinn's Quest

iUniverse books may be ordered through booksellers or by contacting:

iUniverse
1663 Liberty Drive
Bloomington, IN 47403
www.iuniverse.com
1-800-Authors (1-800-288-4677)

ISBN: 978-1-4401-9395-8 (sc)
ISBN: 978-1-4401-9397-2 (dj)
ISBN: 978-1-4401-9396-5 (ebk)

Printed in the United States of America

iUniverse rev. date: 02/16/2010

Chapter One

Hester Prynne did the nasty with Rev. Dimmesdale because her husband was old, fat and ugly. She forgot to take her birth control pills, so she got preggers and had a little girl. She named the baby Pearl because she liked to knit.

"Lord, help me," Quinn O'Connor grumbled and tossed the essay onto her desk. She set her grading pen next to an open can of diet root beer and massaged her temples. "Jeez, it's already five," she moaned, looking at the clock on the opposite wall.

As she turned to look outside the classroom, sunlight pierced the window and flashed in her face. Blinded, she jerked in the opposite direction knocking over the can of soda. The dark liquid splashed across the desk and onto the tan canvas briefcase beside her chair. She snatched the last wad of tissue from the box next to the stapler and sopped up as much soda as she could.

"Just one more mess in my lousy day."

She stared at a stack of half-finished *Romeo and Juliet* quizzes atop the small filing cabinet beside her desk. "You'd think the administration could give us a heads-up when they're planning a fire drill in the middle of class. Now, I'll have to write a whole new quiz." She pursed her lips and groaned. "And that over-sized dimwit, Billy Marshall, throwing a paper airplane at Mary Elizabeth—what was he thinking? I'm glad I sent him to the principal. Maybe he'll think twice before he pulls a stunt like that again." She leaned back in her chair and sighed. "Thank goodness it's Friday because I need a break from this place."

Disregarding the "preggers" drivel, she grabbed the rest of the student essays and bent down to put them into her soggy briefcase.

Thud. Her head hit the edge of the desk; pain shot across her forehead.

"Ouch!" She kicked the desk, added a few curse words, and stuffed the essays into her open case.

She hustled out of the classroom and headed for the faculty parking lot of John F. Kennedy High School. A warm April breeze brushed her cheeks as she walked. The only vehicle left in the lot was her silver Chevy Tahoe parked at the far end.

"Yep, buying this monster was a good idea, even if it does cost a mint to run," she said, admiring the vehicle as she approached. Smiling, she opened the door of the SUV and pitched her briefcase onto the passenger seat. Thirty essays tumbled into disarray as the unzipped case bounced off the seat and fell onto the floorboard. "Crap!"

She hoisted herself onto the driver's seat and closed the door. Leaning sideways over the center console she reached for the papers, but her arms were too short. Twisting, she sprawled her upper body across the console and pulled her knees onto the driver's seat.

"Just see if you can get away from me now." Using her feet against the door for leverage, she pushed her torso over the console plummeting her head and shoulders into the space between the dashboard and the passenger seat.

Jeez! I think I'm stuck, she told herself.

Teetering upside down with her skirt scrunched around her waist and her panties showing she muttered, "Crap, I hope some student doesn't see me like this."

She crammed the papers into her briefcase and closed the zipper. Wiggling free from the passenger seat abyss she eased herself upright and stuck the key in the ignition.

A hot flash exploded drenching her head and neck with perspiration.

"Crap!" She slammed the palms of her hands against the steering wheel and took two deep breaths. "Five minutes, this will be over in five minutes if I don't move too much." She started the Tahoe, opened the windows, and pulled out of the parking lot.

How much longer am I going to have to feel like dunking my head in a bucket of ice water every time a flash hits? she asked herself. *I've suffered with this for two years. Jeez, I'm almost fifty— isn't it time for this to be over.*

She tried to concentrate on the weekend and having lunch with her best friend, Eddy Baldwin, on Saturday.

I'll call her when I get home and see if she wants to meet at that cute little bistro in Laguna Beach. We can check out the shops afterward. A few blocks ahead she spied the road leading to the mall. *Maybe I should I stop and buy more peppermint candles. No, I think I have enough to last through next week.* She chuckled and ran the fingers of her left hand through her hair to see if it had dried since the flash. *Poor Patrick, he's complained about my peppermint candles ever since I read the article in* Woman's Day *that said peppermint was calming for menopausal women. If I run out, he'll be happy.*

Patrick, her husband, had left for Santa Barbara on Wednesday to negotiate the details of a merger and she did not expect him back until Sunday evening.

Gosh, it seems like he's gone on business more and more lately. I miss his funny laugh and the smell of his pipe.

Quinn turned into her upscale Orange County neighborhood and spied a police car parked in front of her house.

I wonder what kind of mischief the juvenile delinquent next door has gotten himself into this time.

Two officers walked up to meet her as she pulled into the driveway. "Are you Mrs. Patrick O'Connor?" asked the taller one.

"Yes."

"I'm Officer Collins and this is my partner, Officer Trujillo. Can we step inside to talk for a minute?" His tone was somber.

"Ah ... of course," she stammered caught off guard. *This doesn't sound like it has anything to do with a neighborhood prank.* Sweat formed in the palms of her hands as she got out of her car. "Follow me," she said and headed for the front door. She unlocked the house and walked into the living room.

The officers looked a bit uneasy.

"Have a seat," she offered.

They ignored her invitation.

"I'm afraid we have some bad news, Mrs. O'Connor. Your husband has been in an accident," Officer Collins said.

An icy shiver ran down her spine. "Is ... is he okay?"

The officer's brows furrowed. "Unfortunately, he didn't survive."

"Oh, my God!" She gasped for air. "It can't be. I just spoke with him last night. Are you sure it's him?" Beads of moisture exploded on her forehead.

"I'm sorry, ma'am. His identification was in the vehicle."

Quinn's knees buckled and she slumped into Patrick's favorite overstuffed chair.

Officer Collins took out a copy of the accident report. "Your husband's car went over the edge of a grade on Highway 101 just north of Thousand Oaks early this morning. The time of the accident is estimated at 4:00 AM." He looked up from the report. "It seems no one saw the accident, so it wasn't reported for several hours." His eyes skimmed down the report searching for the place where he left off. "Apparently, Mr. O'Connor lost control of the vehicle. It rolled over several times before landing at the bottom of a ravine. Your husband and the passenger were pronounced dead at the scene. We regret we couldn't notify you earlier, ma'am."

"Passenger?" Quinn did not move but her mind was spinning. *Didn't he say he was going alone? Why wasn't he in Santa Barbara where he was supposed to be?* Her throat tightened and her voice quivered as she asked, "Wasn't he by himself?"

"No, ma'am."

"Who … who was with him?"

"The report says the passenger was a Miss Kathy Sullivan."

The color drained from Quinn's face as she pictured the long legs and big boobs of the stunning young attorney. "Kathy was with him?"

"Yes, ma'am." Collins looked down at her. "Are you all right, Mrs. O'Connor? Can I get you some water? Would you like us to call someone?"

"No," she murmured. "I'm okay."

"Someone from the Ventura County Medical Examiner's Office will call you later concerning your plans for the remains," Officer Trujillo said.

"What?"

The officer repeated the information and explained, "It's not necessary for you to go to Ventura County to identify your husband. A funeral home can arrange to transfer the body down here and you can view the remains then." He placed a business card on the small table next to her. "Call this number if you need any additional information."

"Are you sure you don't want us to contact someone—a family member or friend?" Officer Collins offered again.

"No, I can manage," she said as if in a trance.

The officers left in silence.

Quinn was numb. Her hands began to shake and she dug her fingernails into the arms of the chair.

Patrick is dead.

Kathy was with him.

She drew in a ragged breath and shuddered. *That conniving slut set her eyes on my Patrick the moment she walked into his law firm—strutting around the office in her tight skirts and four-inch heels, pretending to be a lady.*

"I saw right through you, bitch!"

There's only one reason Patrick wasn't in Santa Barbara—one reason he was with her at four in the morning. Lurching out of the chair she turned and gave it two violent kicks.

"That's one for each of you, bastards!"

The twenty-six year old wedding portrait on the mantel zoomed into focus. Quinn's facial muscles tightened. She clenched her teeth. Hot tears stung as she marched to the fireplace, picked up the picture, and stared at her husband's face.

"How could you do this to me?" she screamed.

Staggering backward she hurled the wedding portrait against the stone hearth. Her body convulsed in sobs and she sank to the floor amid shards of glass.

"What am I going to tell the children?"

Chapter Two

Three months later

Quinn closed the refrigerator door. "It looks like everything is out of here." She turned to Eddy. "Is my quilt in the car?"

"Yes," her friend replied, "right next to the carton of peppermint candles." Eddy picked up a plastic crate of books from the kitchen table and groaned under its weight. "Do you want these in the trailer or the car?"

"The trailer."

"Tell me honestly, do you think you're going to read all these?"

"That's my intention—rest, read and relax." Quinn smiled and rubbed her hands on the sides of her faded jeans. "You were right about me needing to get away from here for a while. Thank goodness, Uncle Sean offered his place in New Mexico." She opened and closed cupboard doors searching for items she wanted to take with her.

"How long are you planning to be gone?" Eddy set the box of books on the kitchen island and wiped sweat off her brow with the back of her hand.

"I don't know, at least a few months—maybe longer. He told me I could use the house as long as I wanted."

"Is Megan still upset about you going to New Mexico?"

"What do you think?" Quinn sat on a stool next to the counter. "She was pretty direct when she called Saturday. Her closing comment was, 'I don't know why you want to uproot your life like this.' She doesn't understand my life's already been wrenched up by its roots."

Eddy gave her friend a reassuring hug. "She'll come around."

"I'm not so sure. She's convinced it's too dangerous for me to be alone in a strange place. Megan seems to have conveniently forgotten she was alone when she moved to Philadelphia. She thinks I'm a decrepit old person who can't be trusted to look out for myself."

"Oh, give the kid a break. She loves her mother. Where's the crime in that?"

"I know I should be grateful to have kids who care about me. It's just now that Megan and Rick are adults, sometimes they can be so exasperating."

Eddy smiled. "Can't control them, can you?"

The next morning before sunrise, Quinn backed her Tahoe and small trailer out of the driveway. She took one last look at her house through the dim light of predawn and began the journey to New Mexico.

This is the right thing to do. I know it is. If I stick around here, I'm never going to find myself again.

She headed inland toward the desert and did not stop until she reached the Barstow Station McDonalds. She wandered around the station's old rail car shops looking at trinkets and souvenirs. A pack of playing cards with the Hollywood sign on the back caught her eye. Her stomach growled and she circled back to the food area without making a purchase.

At the main counter, she bought a breakfast sandwich and orange juice. In a passenger car dining area crowded with early morning travelers, she slid into an empty booth near the back and took her time eating.

Starting out again, she drove down the long slope of highway leading to the Mojave Desert.

If I keep a steady pace, I can make it across before the temperature gets too hot. She set the cruise control on 65 miles per hour. The monotony of the desert soon cleared her mind and she began to relax.

She reached for the radio dial but pulled her hand back. *Quiet is what I need.*

Quinn's SUV emerged from the Mojave in the early afternoon and began the approach to Flagstaff. The temperature cooled as she drove up the mountain. She rolled down the driver's side window, inhaled deeply, and closed her eyes for a moment.

Mmm, I love the smell of pine trees.

In Flagstaff, she turned off the interstate onto a state highway. She thought about stopping for lunch but decided to forge ahead. Log homes dotting the landscape caught her attention as she neared the edge of town.

It might be fun to live in one of those. I wonder if Uncle Sean's place is a log home.

The terrain became barren when the narrow highway reached the base of the mountain and entered the Navajo Nation.

Before long, she reached the Old Cameron Trading Post by the Little Colorado River. The timeworn building was a welcome sight. Her legs ached and she needed to stretch. She parked near the entrance and stepped out of the SUV.

"Wow!" She winced as a powerful punch of July air hit her in the face. "Is it always this hot out here?" she asked a gray-haired woman dressed in a traditional Navajo velvet skirt and blouse.

The old lady nodded and continued hobbling toward a green Chevy pickup.

Quinn entered the front door of the trading post. A wide array of merchandise from expensive jewelry and fine art to cheap curios filled the building.

"Do you sell food here?" she asked a Native American woman standing behind a display case full of turquoise necklaces. "I'm dying for an ice-cold drink and something to eat."

"We have a nice restaurant back there," the woman said, turning and pointing to an entryway at the rear of the store. "And there's a small grocery area in the back of the other side of the store."

Quinn found just what she was looking for at the small grocery mart—a diet root beer and a hot dog. She perched on a bench outside the building and wolfed down her lunch. A few minutes later, she was back on her way.

Yellow canopies on the roadside near Tuba City sheltered venders selling locally made jewelry.

"I should have bought a turquoise ring or something at the trading post," she lamented and parked in front of the first canopy. After examining all the silver rings in the various booths, she purchased one with lapis, turquoise and malachite inlay. She slipped it on the middle finger of her right hand and smiled. "Not bad."

She popped a rock 'n' roll oldies disc into the CD player and cranked up the volume as she drove down the highway. Tapping her fingers on the steering wheel in time to the music she admired the glint of her new ring as it caught the sunlight through the front window. Bobby Vee's rendition of *Devil or Angel* blared and she sang along without missing a beat.

There's something about that song. The lyrics have a habit of popping into my head at the oddest times—even at the hairdresser.

Driving deeper into Indian country, the stark whiteness of the clouds against the intense blue of the sky presented a sharp contrast to the dulling smog that often hung over Southern California.

A person can breathe out here.

Ancient mesas lined the side of the highway. *They look like remnants of a mighty civilization worn away by the erosion of thousands of years. I bet they hide a lot of secrets.*

She rounded a curve and on a small rise near the highway spied a Navajo weaver working at her loom under a brush-covered shelter. *Jeez, it must take months to weave one of those rugs. No wonder they were so expensive at the trading post.*

Arroyos devoid of water slithered back and forth under the road as she pressed on.

Soon the edge of Monument Valley peeked out from behind the sleepy village of Kayenta.

She stopped at the local Burger King to get a drink. Sitting in a booth sipping on a diet soda her pent-up emotions broke loose. Tears formed in the corners of her eyes as she remembered the looks on her children's faces when she told them the circumstances of their father's death. Both Rick and Megan tried to make excuses for him.

"Maybe the whole thing was innocent. Maybe he really was on business," they had said.

In the end, she was sure they realized the truth. She lowered her head to hide her tears from the other patrons and rushed outside to her SUV. After a few minutes, she regained her composure and continued on her way.

Near the New Mexico border more tears exploded.

How could my Patrick have turned into such a cheating bastard? Maybe all men are bastards at heart. There's no way in hell he should have gotten away with cheating on me.

Twice she pulled off the road to dry her eyes.

The mauve hand of evening had not touched the horizon when she arrived in the Northwest New Mexico town of Farmington.

I thought this place was going to be brown and dusty but look at all the trees and flowers.

Quinn knew Farmington was one of the largest cities in New Mexico, but to her surprise it turned out to be only a medium-sized town. Still, there were many familiar businesses like Red Lobster, Best Buy, Home Depot, and Sears.

"This is just large enough to have everything I need, but small enough it's not packed with people," she said feeling energized. "I'm going to like living here—at least for a while."

A short drive later, she arrived at Uncle Sean's vacation home. Quinn had never been there but she knew it was her uncle's favorite getaway before his health began to decline. The house was located on a small bluff overlooking the San Juan River.

She parked in the gravel driveway and turned off the engine. *It's good to finally get here.* She took a quick survey of the place through the front windshield.

The traditional pueblo style home was painted dark terra cotta.

It's not a log cabin, but the place has style, she thought, admiring the weathered iron gate at the entrance to a walled courtyard in front of the house.

She got out of the vehicle and walked to the back of the house. From the deck, she could see the river at the bottom of the cliff. Shades of green and yellow from the cottonwood trees blended with reflections of beige from the riverbank as the setting sun shone on the water.

It's so peaceful here.

She strolled back to the courtyard, slid the bolt aside and pushed the heavy gate open.

Clang, rang the cowbell attached to the gate.

Peeking inside she saw two red and yellow folk art chairs sitting beside a dark blue ceramic birdbath. She stepped through the gate into the patio. Colorful pots lining the walls were filled with columbine, daisies, and desert marigolds turning the area into a tranquil garden.

Uncle Sean said he'd have the place ready for me, guess he wasn't kidding.

Quinn opened her purse and fetched the key to the roughly hewn wooden front door. She unlocked the door and walked inside. A bright kitchen branched off the right side of the small entryway. Straight ahead was a cozy living room with a fireplace and French doors that opened onto the deck. There was a hall on the right side of the living room leading to an office, a bathroom and two bedrooms.

"This feels like home," she said walking through the retreat.

It was dark before Quinn finished unloading her belongings.

Later that evening, she sat on the living room floor surrounded by boxes. A peppermint candle burned on a small plate in front of her. She savored its fumes. For the first time, in a long time, her body felt completely calm. Gone were the fluttering waves of anxiety that had plagued her since Patrick's death.

"Now what?" she whispered.

Chapter Three

Early the next morning Quinn rolled out of bed and caught a glimpse of her faded blue pajamas in the full-length mirror on the back of the bedroom door. "Maybe I should get dressed," she moaned. "Oh, who the heck is going to see me?"

She made a quick trip to the bathroom then plodded up the short hallway. The walls were covered with photos of her uncle and his fishing buddies holding their prized trout. Patrick smiled out from two of the photographs.

"I don't want to look at *your* face every day I'm here." She removed Patrick's photos and placed them on the closet self in the spare bedroom.

Walking back into the living room, she made a mental note to hang the pictures back up before going home. Distracted, she bumped her toe on the plate holding the peppermint candle from the night before.

"Crap," she groused. "Mom always said I needed to learn to pick up after myself." Boxes of her belongings cluttered the room. "Where do I start?"

She spied her special quilt tossed on top of a box near the French doors. Grandmother Maguire had given the Irish chain quilt to Quinn on her fourteenth birthday. The enclosed note said, "Whenever you are lonely or sad, cuddle up and remember you are loved."

Tears formed. "I miss you so much, Grandma." She picked up the worn cover and held it tight. It had helped her through many difficult times, especially the last few months.

She opened the French doors and a gust of cool air whipped inside. Wrapping herself in the quilt she walked out onto the deck and stopped by the railing.

Patrick probably stood in this same spot last year. She shuddered and tightened her fingers around the frayed edge of the quilt pulling it closer.

Two fly fishermen wading in the river below reminded her of the times Patrick had asked her to go fishing. *I should have fessed up to the real reason I wouldn't go fishing with him—I never could see the challenge in outsmarting a fish."*

She walked along the railing and pondered a telephone conversation she had with Uncle Sean during Patrick's last fishing trip.

Uncle Sean's voice quivered when he told me Patrick was in town .... his voice never quivers. Maybe I should have been more suspicious about what Patrick was really snagging while he was here, or if he was here at all.

Quinn spent the next two weeks unpacking and putting the house in order.

Each afternoon she drove three miles to the post office. After picking up her mail, she often stopped at the small convenience store next door. Today as she approached the building, a poster in the window advertising the Animas Spa and Fitness Center caught her attention.

"Hum ... just the place to lose this flab." She pinched the extra ring of fat around her waist and grimaced before going inside to purchase a diet root beer.

Back home, she rummaged through a couple of unpacked boxes in her bedroom searching for the workout clothes she packed on a lark. Assorted items flew into a disheveled heap on the floor. At the bottom of the second box, a purple leotard and matching tights materialized.

I wonder if these still fit. I haven't worn them in years. She wiggled into the outfit and stared at herself in the bedroom mirror. Her face twisted into a scowl.

"Jeez, I look like a giant grape that's about to burst. I need to buy some new exercise clothes before going to the fitness center."

Two days later, Quinn waltzed into the fitness center ready to take her punishment. The manager, a well-built young man named Hal, swaggered as he showed Quinn through the facility. Decked out in her new light blue sweatpants, matching zippered sweatshirt, and a dark blue tee she followed close behind him. She chuckled to herself as he puffed out his chest preening like a rooster for the women on the exercise equipment.

"Hi, Hal," three young women called in unison. They waved and ogled Hal's body as he passed. He acknowledged their attention with a smile and a thumbs-up.

He does have a cute butt, she thought.

"We have all the best equipment here," he said.

"Oh, I bet you do," she snapped before realizing she was talking out loud.

"What did you say?" He looked over his shoulder at her.

"Ah, I said … isn't that Sue?" She pointed to a heavyset woman on an exercise bike. Quinn's cheeks were on fire and she knew they were turning pink.

"No, I think her name is Vera or Kira, or something like that. Did I tell you, you get one free trial day?"

"Can I take it now?" she asked, pleased he did not seem to notice her blunder.

"Of course, just be sure to sign in at the front desk."

Thirty minutes later, sweat cascaded down Quinn's face and back. She slowed her treadmill to a stop. After staggering off, she meandered over to the water vending machine in the break area.

"Hi. I haven't seen you around here before," a wafer-thin redhead seated at a nearby table said. "Are you new?"

"I'm taking a trial visit." Quinn reached in her pocket, took out a dollar and fifty cents, and put it in the vending machine.

"Why don't you come over and sit with us?" the woman said, fluffing her hair. She patted an empty chair next to a pudgy blonde sporting a beehive hairdo that looked like it was left over from the 60's.

They seem friendly enough. Besides, my legs are killing me. Quinn carried her bottle of water to the table and took a seat

"I'm Linda Lou Purdy, and this is my friend Bunny Randall," the redhead offered. "We're regulars, never miss a Tuesday or Thursday."

"I'm Quinn O'Connor. It's nice to meet you."

"Are you from around here, Quinn?" Bunny asked and adjusted her silver-rimmed eyeglasses.

"No. I'm from California. I've only been here a couple of weeks."

"Has anyone warned you?" Linda Lou asked. "You need to be sure to use sunscreen, sweetie. The ultra-violet rays at this altitude will ruin your complexion. I have some friends whose faces are dried up like prunes because they weren't careful."

The small talk continued and Linda Lou deftly moved the conversation to the quality of eligible men in town.

"Some of the good old boys are great, but a lot of them are scoundrels," she said.

"You've got to watch out who you associate with," Bunny added.

"Take for instance, my ex-husband," Linda Lou said. "I caught the sumbitch red-handed with our neighbor fifteen years ago. I'd suspected something was going on for a couple of weeks, but you could have knocked me over with a feather when I opened our bedroom door. There he was in all his glory," her eyes misted and her voice began to tremble, "not with the woman next door, but with the *man* next door."

Bunny seemed to sense how much the incident still cut to the quick and shifted the subject to her own failed marriage.

"You know how it goes. You get to be a certain age and add a few pounds. Then some cute young thing catches your husband's eye. Before you know it, everything goes kablooey and you're all alone." Bunny smacked the table with her fist and her glasses slid down the bridge of her nose. "But, by God, he didn't get off cheap." She pushed the glasses back with her index finger and posed with an air of triumph.

"That's right. Bob Randall paid a pretty price for his little chippie," Linda Lou said. "Bunny is set for life. Aren't you?"

"I'm A-OK," Bunny said with a wide grin.

"By the way, Quinn, what brings you to New Mexico?" Linda Lou asked. "Not man trouble, I hope?"

"No. Not really. My husband died in an accident a couple of months ago. I just needed to get away for a while." Quinn didn't feel like joining the husband bashing—at least not yet.

"I'm so sorry," Bunny touched Quinn's hand. "It must be hard to lose a husband that way."

Linda Lou nodded sympathetically. "Bunny and I are going to Jake's Place for a few drinks tomorrow night. It's a little spot not too far from here. Would you like to join us? It would give you a chance to meet some new people and get your mind off of your situation. Do you think you're up to it, sweetie?"

Quinn grinned. "Sounds like a great idea."

A mass of people huddled near the door waiting for tables at Jake's. Inside, country music blasted. Quinn made her way through the crowd and found Linda Lou and Bunny in a corner booth near the dance floor.

"I can't believe this place. It's packed," Quinn said and slid into the booth beside Bunny.

"Hey, it's Friday night. Check out the possibilities." Linda Lou made a large sweeping gesture as if offering the men on a platter.

A petite waitress appeared. "The gentleman at the table over there would like to buy you ladies a drink. What can I get you?"

"I've been out of circulation a long time. Is it okay to accept?" Quinn asked Linda Lou.

"Sweetie, never turn down a free drink. We'll have margaritas."

"And now, the games begin," Bunny chuckled. "That's Davis buying our drinks, he loves the ladies. Let's see who he's after tonight."

A tall, muscular man dressed in cowboy attire and carrying a beer approached their booth. Quinn thought he looked about fifty but his cowboy hat made it difficult to tell for sure. She remembered Eddy's warning about men wearing hats—they're probably bald.

"Mind if I sit down?" he asked in a Texas drawl and tipped his Stetson.

"Have a seat," Linda Lou patted on the cushion beside her.

"How are you ladies doing tonight?" He moved smoothly into the booth and looked across the table. "Hi there, Bunny honey," he said, giving her a wink. His gaze turned to Quinn. "I haven't seen you around these parts before, darlin'. What's your name?"

"Quinn." Her stomach turned at the sight of his gold wedding band.

"Well, Quinn, nice to meet you."

"She's only here temporarily," Bunny offered and adjusted her glasses.

"You on vacation or something?" he asked.

"I'm on a sort of sojourn."

"Sojourn ... how interesting." He paused to take a swig of beer. "Say, little lady, what are you doing tomorrow night?"

Quinn stiffened. "I have plans."

The temperature inside Jake's was rising and she pulled on the collar of her blouse to counter the stifling heat.

Crap, it's a hot flash!

Perspiration formed at her hairline. "I'm sorry, I have to leave," she said and scooted to the edge of the seat.

"But you just got her, sweetie," Linda Lou wrinkled her brow. "Can't you stay a little longer?"

"I apologize but I'm not feeling well. I'll see you on Tuesday." She gave the Texan a weak smile and slipped out of the booth. Walking away she overheard Davis talking to Linda Lou.

"That's one fine-looking woman. Did you notice how she blushed when I spoke to her? She wants me. Hey, what's a sojourn, anyhow?"

Quinn drove home with the car windows open, but despite the cool summer air she could not shake her dark mood. She envisioned Davis' unsuspecting wife waiting for his return. She remembered Linda Lou and Bunny talking about their ex-husbands. She thought about Patrick.

Cheating pieces of slime—all of them, just cheating pieces of slime! For years I sacrificed my career to take care of Patrick and the children. And what was my reward? The conniving scoundrel cheated on me with a younger woman.

Looking back, she was certain Patrick had been with Kathy and a long way from Santa Barbara when he called home the night before the fatal crash.

"Going over the details of a business merger, my ass!" she barked. "It was a merger all right, but not the legal kind." She tried to stay focused on the hilly road but tears clouded her eyes. "Patrick, you bastard!"

The signs were there—I should have noticed. He was out of town more often. He was tired when he got home and didn't want to make love. Well, he probably was exhausted, considering what he'd been up to. How could I have been so stupid?"

She took a tissue from the center console and dabbed her eyes.

After the accident, it seemed to Quinn like everyone had known about Patrick's affair with Kathy Sullivan except her. Crushed and embarrassed she turned to her best friend.

"I don't know what I'd do without your friendship—probably wallow in misery," she told Eddy.

Almost nightly the two women met to drink wine, munch on cheese, and commiserate about philandering husbands.

One evening Quinn came up with a theory. "What is it the mother in *Moonstruck* says? Something about men chasing women because they fear death? Maybe that's why Patrick cheated on me." She took the last sip from her wineglass and waited for Eddy's response.

"Hell, no! They cheat because they can." Eddy reached for the bottle and refilled their glasses.

"You're right. There's always some young thing willing to spread her legs for a crack at becoming a trophy wife." Quinn took a large gulp of wine and let out a thundering belch.

Eddy choked and a piece of cheese flew out of her mouth. The women burst into laughter.

"It's good to hear you laugh again," Eddy said. "Do you remember what I did when I caught my first husband cheating? I took him to the cleaners. Women shouldn't have to put up with shit like that from men."

A deer ran across the isolated road jolting Quinn back from her memories. She hit the brakes and narrowly missed the animal. Regaining her wits, she stomped on the accelerator. The

Tahoe hesitated for an instant before shifting gears and lurching forward. Her eyes narrowed and a slight smile crossed her lips.

"I'll show you, Patrick. There's no way you're keeping *me* down."

Chapter Four

Quinn decided to abandon the local bar scene for a while after her experience at Jake's Place. The next Friday night, she stayed home and watched television.

Wiggling into the corner of the living room sofa she reached for the remote control and clicked on the preview screen. The sports channel had NASCAR racing—not what she had in mind. The news on CNN was too depressing. Scrolling farther down she found a romantic comedy, *Inspired by a Kiss*, on TMC—just what she needed. She punched in the channel, took a gulp of diet root beer, and soon lost herself in the film.

Roger, the handsome leading man, looked to be in his mid-forties while Allison playing opposite him was stunning and considerably younger. An intriguing relationship was developing between the two.

ALLISON: My father left this business to me, and I certainly don't need you telling me what will be next season's most kissable lipstick color.
ROGER: Look, you may be Jack's daughter but you have no experience in the cosmetic industry.
ALLISON: What do you mean by no experience? I've been the face of this company for the last five

years. I know more about lipstick in one lip than
you do in that whole swollen head of yours.

ROGER: Well, let's see.

*Roger bent forward, wrapped one arm around
Allison's waist, and swept her to him pressing his lips
against hers. She struggled, but only for a moment.
Looking into his blue eyes, she smiled.*

ALLISON: Apparently, your head isn't your only
body part that's swollen.

ROGER: Apparently, not.

*He lifted Allison into his arms and carried her to
the black leather sofa near windows overlooking the
Manhattan skyline. Without warning, he dropped
her onto the couch.*

ALLISON: Hey, quit kidding around.

ROGER: Do I look like I'm kidding?

Quinn's eyes never left the screen. He lowered his body on
top of Allison. His mouth caressed her eyes, her cheeks, her lips,
and neck. He unbuttoned her blouse. His head descended and
disappeared from view. Allison bit her bottom lip and closed her
eyes.

Quinn's mouth opened slightly—her nipples ached—her
hips tilted forward—her body opened and throbbed.

"Omigod," she whispered, "Patrick never set me off so
quickly."

The plot blurred into the background as she fixated on the
man behind the role. *Who is he? How can an actor affect me like
that?*

She searched the credits at the end of the film. *There he is—
Sam Maxwell.*

On Saturday, consumed by images of Sam Maxwell, Quinn
put the silverware in the refrigerator.

On Sunday, she went to church and had sinful thoughts about Sam Maxwell.

On Monday, she called the teller at the bank "Sam" and couldn't remember why she was in line.

And, so went the next few days.

Thursday evening she sat in the courtyard with her feet propped on a large, empty terra cotta pot. The air was crisp and stars punctuated the sky like specks of glitter.

"What has happened to me?" she shouted at the sky. "I used to be a mature, sensible person. Now, all I can think about is *him.* This is not how a mother of grown children should behave."

She lowered her feet and gave the terra cotta pot a swift kick. "He was playing a part, just a part. He's probably a real jerk. Get a grip. Get a life!"

The next morning Quinn sat at the kitchen table in her pajamas. She held a diet breakfast drink in one hand and rubbed her forehead with the other.

"Why can't I stop thinking about Sam Maxwell?" she mumbled. "Am I crazy?"

She stared at the diet drink and considered bingeing on scrambled eggs, bacon, and chocolate milk. "I will not eat out of frustration," she repeated over and over while finishing her breakfast drink.

Shopping will clear my mind. She got up from the table and headed down the hall to change her clothes.

The mall in Farmington could fit into one corner of the South Coast Plaza where she usually shopped. Still, she was determined to find something interesting. Two clothing stores, a jewelry store, and a discount shoe store later, she was singing to herself in the middle of a Hallmark store.

I wonder if they have the angels Eddie collects.

"I'm sorry ma'am but we don't carry that brand," a tall sales clerk replied when Quinn asked about them.

As she left the store, Quinn's stomach emitted a thundering rumbled. She glanced at her watch. *Jeez, it's noon. No wonder my stomach is growling. I'd better get something to eat before I embarrass myself.*

At the edge of the food court, she ran into Bunny.

"Hi, fancy meeting you here," Bunny said in her cheery voice and threw a hot fudge sundae container in a trash receptacle. "What are you up to?"

"I'm just grabbing a bite to eat. Want to sit down and catch up on things?"

"Sorry, I … I can't stay. I have to go." Bunny opened her purse, fumbled around and pulled out her car keys.

"Is everything okay?" Quinn asked.

"Oh, I'm just late for ah … ah, for lunch. Really, everything is A-OK." Bunny adjusted her glasses and hurried off.

Strange—why was she eating ice cream if she hadn't had lunch? Oh, well.

"I'll have a turkey sandwich on wheat with all the veggies," Quinn told the sandwich maker at the Subway.

"Should I make that a meal?" the cashier asked before ringing up her order.

"No, just the sandwich and a bottle of water," she said proud of herself for resisting the urge to add a bag of chips and a cookie.

After lunch, Quinn headed across the street to Wal-Mart. Wandering down the massive candy aisle, she spotted one of her favorites—cans of foil-wrapped, butter crunch toffee covered with chocolate and almonds.

They're only small cans, she rationalized and snatched one off the shelf. She put it in her cart and sped down the aisle before she could change her mind.

She turned the corner and a huge display of DVDs stood in the middle of her path. "I can't believe it," she said coming face-to-face with a copy of *Inspired by a Kiss*. "It must be destiny." Without hesitation, she plucked it from the display and tossed it into the cart beside the toffee. "A perfect pair," she said heading for the checkout counter and home.

Quinn tried to wedge her fingernail through the shrink-wrapped cover of the DVD. "Crap! These things are impossible to open."

She pulled a pair of scissors from the kitchen drawer and poked at the plastic, but the point was too dull to puncture the wrapper. Rooting around, she found a paring knife buried under an egg slicer at the bottom of the drawer.

"This will do it," she said, punching the tip of the knife into the plastic and freeing the disc.

She scurried into the living room, inserted the disc into the DVD player by the television, and plopped down on the sofa.

"Now, let's see what happens." She picked up the remote and fast-forwarded to the crucial scene.

Sam unbuttoned "Allison's" blouse, his lips skimmed down her neck, and his head disappeared from sight.

Quinn's body pulsed—her heart pounded—her breath quickened. She lost sense of place and time.

"Holy mackerel!" She leaned her head against the back of the sofa. "I haven't felt like that since …" she could not remember.

For twenty-six years she had considered her marriage to Patrick solid.

Sure, the passion lessened but there was always love between us. Wasn't there? Or, was I deluding myself? Maybe I was subconsciously aware of his cheating. Maybe that's why I've felt so empty for the last year.

"Patrick, you shit," she said and groused over being traded in for a newer model.

At least once a day for the next five days, she watched the movie. With each viewing she discovered new things about Sam Maxwell.

His jaw was strong and angular with a small scar on the bottom of his chin. Quinn's cousin had fallen off his skateboard when he was ten and suffered a similar gash.

Was that what happened to Sam? Maybe a jealous husband punched him. Maybe he was hit in the chin by a flying beer bottle in a barroom brawl.

Sam's Barrymore nose was perfect and below it he sported a meticulous mustache. His smile was slightly crooked.

That's probably the reason for the mustache. But he wouldn't look as sexy without it. Strange—I've never found mustaches sexy before.

His long fingers reminded her of a pianist. When the camera closed in she realized he was a nail biter.

Each time she watched the other love scene near the end of the movie her eyes followed his thicket of chest hair as it trailed past his navel. Each time erotic desire arose.

"How can I hunger for a man I've never even met?" she chided herself after each viewing.

The next Friday Quinn refused Linda Lou's invitation for dinner at Jake's. Instead she ate a tuna salad sandwich in the courtyard.

Sitting in the wooden chair next to the birdbath she enjoyed the mild evening breeze. She inhaled the fragrance of the flowers and relaxed until time for her favorite late night show.

"Welcome. Welcome everyone to *The Goodnight Show*. It's nice to have you here." The studio audience applauded and Hayes Bello launched into his monologue.

She relaxed and enjoyed the fun. As far as she was concerned, it was not bedtime until the show was over. At least, not until after Hayes finished his monologue.

"We'll be right back after the break with the award-winning actor Sam Maxwell."

Did I hear him right? Quinn struggled to catch her breath. Leaning forward she tapped her foot nervously until the show resumed.

"My first guest tonight is the terrific actor, Sam Maxwell, soon to start filming a new action-packed western," Hayes announced.

The lanky actor strode onto the set and shook hands with the host. He unbuttoned his perfectly tailored sport coat and took his place in the guest chair. Maxwell was dressed completely in shades of gray—sport coat, shirt, slacks, and shoes. The monochromatic attire emphasized his blue eyes and silver hair.

Silver hair? His hair was brown in the movie. Still, I love the way he looks.

Quinn felt a hot flash coming on. "Oh, please. Not now," she murmured.

Hayes was engrossed in the interview. "Well Sam, I hear you're off to New Mexico this week to work on your new film, *Turquoise Trail,* with director James Canyon."

"Yes. I'm looking forward to working with James again. He's a wonderful director. We worked together several years ago on the film *Twilight Surprise.*"

Quinn reached for her diet root beer to stave off the heat. *Maybe this isn't a hot flash at all. Maybe it's a reaction to Sam. I don't know which is worse.*

"I remember that film. It won critical acclaim at the Cannes Film Festival, didn't it?" Hayes asked.

"Yes. We were pleased with the recognition. You know, Marina Martinelli will be co-starring in *Turquoise Trail.* I can't wait to work with her."

"I bet you can't." Hayes smirked, hunched his shoulders, and gave a little chuckle. "The lovely Marina Martinelli—half the audience would love to work with her. Wouldn't you, guys?"

As the interview continued Quinn decided Sam Maxwell was a nice guy, not at all full of himself like so many actors.

He's coming to New Mexico. That's unreal.

The sun streamed into the kitchen the next morning illuminating dust motes floating in the air. Through the window Quinn saw two hummingbirds hovering over the marigolds in the courtyard. School had started back home, but in New Mexico her September morning was stress free.

I'm so glad I decided to take a year off. I can't wait to see the colors start to change—they never change in Southern California.

She turned and faced the array of books on the shelf above the kitchen table. *How about* Bless Me Ultima? *It takes place in New Mexico.* She grabbed the novel off the shelf, took a can of diet breakfast drink from of the fridge, and walked out onto the deck.

Sitting on the edge of the comfy chaise lounge she watched for a minute as a blue heron preened itself near the river's edge.

Quinn settled back onto the lounge and opened the novel. Four pages later, shrill squawks filled the sky interrupting her concentration.

Splat! A blue jay deposited his cargo inches from her head.

"Oh crap!" She jumped up and laughed at the accuracy of her observation. "That's a sure sign I shouldn't be out here this morning."

Quinn trotted inside and grabbed her purse. She headed for her car and drove the short distance to the post office.

Inside her mailbox was a copy of the Albuquerque newspaper and a postcard from Eddy who was vacationing in the Bahamas.

Plastered across the front of the postcard was a muscular young man in skimpy swimming trunks. On the flip side was written, "Missing you, girlfriend."

"I miss you, too," she said, "and I hope you come for a visit soon."

Quinn placed the provocative postcard on the message board next to the refrigerator.

"You, young man, will be my incentive to lose weight." She poured herself a glass of water and sat at the kitchen table to read the newspaper.

There wasn't much news. So, even though Patrick had left her more than enough money to live on, she turned to the employment section of the classifieds just for the heck of it.

"Let's see what's available ... nothing but a parade of boring jobs—general laborer, forklift operator, hotel maids, movie extras—movie extras!" She read faster, "Movie extras, all ages needed for a major motion picture. Contact the New Mexico Film Office."

I wonder if this is Sam's film? The newspaper fell to the table and her heart pounded.

In less than a minute, Quinn was seated at her computer in Sean's office. Her fingers flew across the keyboard. A quick search of the Internet found the New Mexico Film Office. She clicked on "Bulletin Board." There it was.

Turquoise Trail—a western, directed by James Canyon. Starring Sam Maxwell and Marina Martinelli. Extras needed, all ages. Report to casting on Monday at 5:00 AM. Fry's Movie Ranch, twenty miles north of Albuquerque on I-25.

Quinn tapped her fingers on the desk. "Oh, heck. Why not?"

Chapter Five

Quinn stood in line with a herd of potential extras in the parking lot of Fry's Movie Ranch on Monday morning. Three young casting assistants walked back and forth scrutinizing the group and stopped a few yards away from Quinn.

Jeez, they look like lizards posing for effect, she said to herself. *I'll bet bulging eyeballs lurk behind their black sunglasses.*

She turned to the diminutive older woman next to her. "That little guy could pass for one of my high school students. How can such juveniles be in charge of our fate?"

The woman shrugged her shoulders.

Quinn tried to appear nonchalant, but noticed the reptilian heads of the casting assistants bobbing in her direction.

A long-limbed, gaunt member of the trio walked over to her. "Come with me, sugar," he said.

"Me?" Quinn's knees wobbled.

"Yes, sugar—you." He grabbed her information card and gave it a quick appraisal. With a wave of his limp wrist he motioned for her to follow him.

Sugar? Who does he think he's calling sugar? I could be his mother!

The unlikely couple took a circuitous path to the wardrobe building. By the time they arrived Quinn's indignation had cooled.

"She's perfect for the preacher's wife," the young casting assistant told the wardrobe mistress. "Get her ready and send her over to the set."

Peering over tiny spectacles the woman took stock of Quinn. "Size twelve dress, size nine shoes?"

"That's right," Quinn replied. "Boy, you're good."

The woman pulled a dress off a nearby rack. "You would be too if you'd been at this for thirty years, sugar." She bent over and picked up a pair of shoes from the floor.

Sugar? Jeez, does everyone around here call people sugar?

Quinn dressed in a jiffy and rushed to the assembly line in the makeup department. Within minutes, she was outside the main set area standing beside an elderly man dressed as a preacher.

Hmm. I think we look quite pious carrying our fake Bibles.

She studied the old man's stooped posture and wrinkled face.

Either he has a very young wife, or I look a lot older than I thought. I'll just pretend I'm his daughter.

"Townspeople, take your places along the side of the street," the assistant director called over a microphone. "When the director calls for action, stroll along or stop and talk in small groups. Don't pay any attention to the men riding in on horses."

Quinn and the preacher waited in front of the Loose Lady Saloon.

After a short delay, the director shouted, "Action!"

The townspeople began to visit and amble along the street.

Maybe Sam will be one of the men on horseback.

Two cowboys on sturdy quarter horses headed toward the bank.

I'll just peek at the riders' reflections on the saloon window as they go by. That way I can see if Sam's one of them, but no one will know what I'm doing.

She turned and looked at the window.

Instead of a reflection she saw Sam Maxwell's blue eyes staring back at her from inside the window.

Her heart hammered. *Ba-boom! Ba-boom! Ba-boom!*

"O … omigod!"

Springing backward, she stumbled on the preacher's size twelve feet. Her body wobbled. She tried to regain her balance by taking two backward steps. The heel of her antique shoe gave way, and she slide off the edge of the plank sidewalk.

"Crap," she yelled.

Everything turned into slow motion as her body tumbled backward.

Splash! She landed smack-dab in the middle of the horse trough in front of the saloon. Cold water jolted her back into real time.

"Cut! Cut!" the director yelled. "Get that woman off my set!"

Quinn's rear sunk to the bottom of the trough. Her legs waved in the air with the heel of her left shoe missing. Something bumped against her shoulder.

The Bible—it's still floating. At least, I won't have to answer for sinking the Word of God.

Her bulky dress and multiple petticoats soaked up half of the water in the trough.

"Help! I can't get up," she cried. "This dress weighs a ton."

Two burly production assistants grabbed her arms and attempted to pull her out, but her wet skin slipped through their fingers.

"Get me out of here!" She flailed about in the trough.

"Stop thrashing lady," the taller man said. "We'll get you out."

Bending over for more leverage, the men tried a second time. Slowly, her body began to emerge from the water.

"I'm slipping, I'm slipping!"

The men lost their grip and she fell back into the trough.

"We need to try something different, Bruno," the shorter production assistant said. "Hold on, lady."

"Let's try this." Bruno extended a massive forearm and placed it under her armpit. The other man did the same and they lifted her out of the water.

Someone threw a blanket around her shoulders and hustled her away from the shooting area. Standing alone next to a fake tree, her teeth chattered and she could not stop shivering.

"Over here, lady," Bruno called from a golf cart. "I'm going to take you to the first aid station, so the doc can check you out."

Quinn hobbled aboard and they sped off.

Bruno stopped in front of an old brick building and helped Quinn from the cart.

"I'll tell the receptionist what happened," he said and hurried inside.

Quinn limped into the building on her broken shoe.

Jeez, I'm a mess. Dripping clothes, dripping hair and I'll bet my makeup is dripping too.

A sweet-faced old nurse handed her a robe. "My goodness, you look a fright. Now, go change into this while we fetch your things from wardrobe. The dressing room is right over there." She pointed to the corner of the room.

Quinn tottered to the little room and changed into the robe. She hung her wet costume on a hook on the back of the door, took off her shoes, and returned to the examining area.

"Hello, young lady. I'm Dr. Navln. How are you doing?" asked a white-haired doctor, who bore an uncanny resemblance to a well-known *Saturday Night Live* alumnus.

"Other than the loss of my dignity and a twisted ankle, there's nothing wrong with me."

"Have a seat over here on the examining table." He patted the table as if inviting a cat to jump up to a perch. "Now, let's take a look at that ankle. I'm told you took a nasty fall, missy." The doctor lifted her leg and began examining the injury.

"Ouch!" She flinched as he poked her anklebone.

He continued to prod her ankle inspecting it in great detail. His right hand slowly moved up and grasped her knee. His other hand squeezed her lower leg.

"You have a well-defined calf for a woman your age," he said. "Has anyone told you that your skin is exceptionally smooth?" His fingers inched farther up her leg and touched her inner thigh.

Quinn yanked her leg from his grip and jumped off of the table. Pain shot up her leg as she landed on the floor.

"Ow! Ow! Ow!" She held back tears and her face turned red. "I'm just fine, doctor!" She pulled her lapel farther across her chest and tightened the robe.

"Doc, the lady needs to come with me over to the legal department," Bruno said, returning from wardrobe with Quinn's clothes and purse. "Is she finished here?"

"I certainly am," she answered. "I'll be right with you. Just give me a minute to change." She took her things from Bruno and tromped off to the dressing room.

I'm not spending another moment with that horny old coot who calls himself a doctor.

"The whole thing was my fault," Quinn told the movie company attorney as she entered his office. "I got flustered and didn't pay attention where I was stepping and …"

"Have a seat," he interrupted and showed her to a chair in front of his desk.

She studied his face waiting for a response to her confession.

The lawyer stared back at her. After a slight pause, he went into a longwinded explanation concerning the movie company's position on the broken shoe.

It's like he didn't hear a word I said. She listened to him drone on and tried to figure out what he was up to. *This guy is hard to read. There's not one line or wrinkle anywhere on his face—probably paralyzed by Botox like those other Hollywood types.*

The attorney finished his speech by saying, "We sincerely apologize for the defective shoe." He pushed a sheet of paper across his desk. "If you'll sign this release guaranteeing not to sue Turquoise Trail Production Company, we'll compensate you for your pain with a two-thousand dollar check right now. Plus, you can send us any medical bills you incur later and we'll pay those also."

Quinn leaned back in the chair.

Did I hear him right? How can I refuse?

Quinn sat with her arms folded and sulked as Bruno drove her back to the first aid station to retrieve her purse which she left behind in her haste to leave.

All I wanted was a glimpse of Sam Maxwell, but I made an absolute fool of myself in front of him. And now, I'm not even going to be in the movie.

The thought of the neatly folded check in her pocket gave her some comfort. She remembered the advice she always gave her students.

When things don't go your way, put the situation in perspective. After all, today is just a brief speck of mortification on the continuum of time.

"Thanks for the ride," she called to Bruno as she exited the golf cart.

She peeked into the first aid station before entering. "Thank goodness that jerk Dr. Navin isn't around," she mumbled.

"Can I help you?" asked a young woman seated at a table near the door.

"I'm Quinn O'Connor. I was in an accident on the set. I left my purse in the changing room."

"Oh, are you the one who fell in the water trough?" The woman looked surprised.

"Yes, that's me."

"Oh ... oh, no."

"What's wrong? Don't you have my purse?"

"Oh, no. I mean, yes. I mean, I'm sure your purse is still in the dressing room. It's just that … oh, no." Distress flashed across her face.

"What's the matter?"

The woman's shoulders sagged; she took a deep breath and sighed. "Sam Maxwell was here not ten minutes ago. He wanted to see how you were doing. I told him I didn't know who he was talking about."

"Oh, no." Quinn's voice dropped.

Shortly after noon, Quinn's Tahoe merged with the string of cars in the drive-thru lane at McDonalds just outside of Albuquerque.

"A double cheeseburger, fries, and a strawberry shake. Oh, and add two apple pies," she shouted into the order microphone.

After my morning, I need a mountain of carbs.

She unwrapped her burger, stuffed a couple of fries in her mouth, and pulled onto the highway leading to Farmington.

I was sure seeing Sam Maxwell in person would put an end to this nonsense—no such luck. Lord, help me—I need a sign!

She jammed half an apple pie in her mouth and wiped her face as the filling dripped down her chin.

Thirty miles beyond the little village of Cuba the sky darkened. Lightning crackled and split the sky. Thunder boomed and rain beat a vicious rhythm on the windshield as she continued up a steep grade.

Jeez, I can't see anything.

Cautiously, she edged the Tahoe onto the shoulder of the road and stopped. The temperature inside the car turned chilly. She grabbed her jacket from the backseat, slipped it over her shoulders, and hunkered down behind the steering wheel to wait out the storm.

I sure hope I don't get stranded out here in the middle of nowhere.

A nearby piñon tree, bending under the weight of the deluge, cast ominous shadows on the passenger side window. She shuddered at the sound of water rushing down the hill.

If this is a sign, I get it—forget about Sam Maxwell.

At last, the storm abated and she pulled back onto the highway. Washed by rain the red and brown rock formations along the road appeared more vibrant, and the air smelled fresher. In the distance, clouds feathered into the crevices of the mountains. She topped a summit and spied an electric rainbow arched over the highway in the valley below.

I've never seen a rainbow with intensity like that—it almost looks neon.

One end of the apparition extended far into the distance, but the other seemed permanently planted in a small field along the side of the road.

It can't be possible. It will disappear any minute. After all, it's impossible to find the end of a rainbow, isn't it?

In a subconscious race against the image, she pressed down on the accelerator.

It's still there.

She drove faster and faster.

And then ... she drove under the rainbow.

"Holy mackerel!"

Easing onto the brakes, she pulled to the side of the road. Stepping out of the SUV, she looked behind her. The brilliant colors still beamed over the highway and ended in the field.

"There's my sign," she whispered to herself. "The end of the rainbow—maybe dreams can come true."

Chapter Six

The phone was ringing when Quinn returned from Albuquerque. She unlocked the front door and hurried into the kitchen. Tossing her purse on the counter, she picked up the phone.

"I thought I'd better check on you out there in old New Mexico," Eddy's familiar voice said.

"Aren't you supposed to be in the Bahamas on vacation?" Quinn sat at the kitchen table. She stared at the young man on postcard that was still pinned to her message board.

"I am, but it's raining, so I figured it was a good time to give you a call. How are you holding up?"

"I'm doing okay. I'm beginning to make a dent in the stack of books you thought I'd never read. Hey, I even went to a bar with a couple of women I met at the fitness center."

"Bar? Fitness center? Is this the same Quinn I grew up with? The one who swore she'd never set foot in a gym and can't stand bars. Tell me you at least met a man."

"Only a married one wearing an expensive Stetson hat."

"Was he bald?" Eddy giggled.

"I didn't stick around long enough to find out." Quinn kicked off her shoes, stretched her legs out and wiggled her toes.

"Oh, sometimes you're no fun."

"How's your husband hunting going?" Quinn asked. "That is the reason you went the Bahamas, isn't it? Have you snagged number four yet?"

"Hell, no! I haven't even found out how many men per woman there are here. But I did find out the ratio of flamingos to people is 60 to 1 over on another island. Want me to bring you a plastic one for your yard?"

"Don't mess with me." Quinn paused for a moment. "You know what I'd really like? I'd like you to come for Thanksgiving."

"I've just been waiting for an invitation."

"Great. I can hardly wait. I've got so much to tell you."

"Have the margarita's ready. Got to go, the rain has stopped and I don't want to miss my tour of the colonial villages over on Harbour Island," Eddy said.

"Have fun." Quinn hung up the phone and took a diet root beer from the fridge.

Eddy could not keep focused on the guide's chatter as the tour group wandered through the villages. Her thoughts kept drifting to Quinn.

I sure hope she finds some peace of mind. None of this mess was her fault. That scumbag rubbed me the wrong way from the moment I set eyes on him. He was always more interested in himself than Quinn. Too bad she didn't leave him a long time ago.

That evening in her hotel room Eddy put on her face, sprayed the last strand of her hair into place, and slipped into her silver cocktail dress.

Now, where are my diamond earrings? She searched through her jewelry pouch. *Aha, there you are.* Plucking them from the bottom, she put them on and looked in the mirror. She smiled. *Men always like their sparkle. Maybe tonight will be my lucky night.*

She left her room and took the stairs to the lobby. Across the foyer she heard the sound of a reggae band in the bar near the swimming pool.

Every time I hear those drums, I feel like dancing, she said to herself and tapped out a samba beat with her Manola Blakah pumps as she neared the entrance of the bar.

Inside she slipped into a chair at an empty table close to the band. She ordered a Dirty Martini with two olives from the barmaid and listened to the music.

"Move over, missy," a deep voice boomed from behind her. "You're blocking my view."

Eddy looked over her shoulder and saw an imposing man in his mid-fifties sitting at the table behind her. The man glared, leaned back in his chair, and puffed on his cigar.

"Sorry, I didn't realize I was in your way," she said.

"Well, you are." The man blew a puff of smoke in her face.

"Please, blow your smoke in another direction," she said with more than a touch of irritation. "Cigar smoke doesn't agree with me."

"Guess that's your problem." He drew in another breath and exhaled in her face again. "Why don't you move?"

"You can move." Eddy crossed her arms and legs. "I'm not budging." She lifted her chin, and turned back to face the band.

The man continued blowing smoke over her shoulder, but after a few songs he left.

"I can see why he was alone. Who could stand him?" she uttered under her breath.

Wind roaring outside Eddy's hotel room woke her the next morning. She pulled back the drapes and peeked at her balcony.

"What a mess!" A potted palm had tipped over in the windstorm, rolled across the balcony and smashed the flowerpots against the guardrail. The deck chairs were upended and butted against the palm.

She rushed to turn on the television. Hurricane warnings flashed across the screen.

"A Category 2 storm is brewing in the Atlantic heading straight for the islands. By the time the hurricane reaches landfall it is expected to be a Category 3 storm with winds approaching 120 miles per hour," the voice-over said.

Shit! The islands are in for a pounding. Maybe I can get out of here before the storm hits.

"The full force of the storm is not expected until tomorrow," the voice continued.

Her body relaxed. "I still have time to get to the mainland."

She called the concierge to book a flight off of the island. By eight-thirty she was checked out of the hotel and waiting for the cab she had ordered. For more than half an hour, she paced back and forth across the lobby.

"Finally," she said as a taxi pulled up in front of the building. Her skirt flapping in the wind, she made a beeline for the vehicle followed by a bellboy with her luggage. The driver popped the trunk and held the door to the cab open as she approached.

A tall man wearing a brown rain slicker bounded past her carrying a suitcase in one hand and briefcase in the other. He threw his suitcase in the trunk and jumped into the cab.

Shit! It's that obnoxious cigar-smoking man from the bar. "Hey, you can't have my cab," she yelled. "Get out!"

"It's my cab now, and I'm not budging." He folded his arms across his chest just as Eddy had done the night before. "So be on your way, missy," he said with a dismissive smirk.

"I will not!" She shoved her foot in the back door of the cab. "Put my things in the trunk," she ordered the bellboy and handed him a generous tip.

"What do you think you're doing?" the man asked.

43

Eddy pushed her way into the backseat forcing the man to move over. "I'm taking *my* cab to the airport, and if that isn't where you're going, too bad."

"Shit," the man said and lit up a cigar.

The television monitors in the airport were tuned to CNN. Eddy watched as she waited to board the plane.

"Island evacuation centers will soon be over-flowing as residents of Freeport scramble to find shelter from the approaching hurricane." The young reporter's jacket whipped in the gale-force wind as he spoke. The camera panned past him to gigantic waves rolling high onto the beach. "Local people have expressed shock at the anticipated size of the storm. Though the hurricane season won't be over until the end of November, residents say September storms of this size have been rare until the last few years."

"We were lucky to get these tickets," said a young woman standing next to Eddy at the gate. "The agent told me this will be the last flight out before the hurricane."

"I don't know what I was thinking coming here this time of year," Eddy said.

"I always come during September, and this is the first time I've been caught in a hurricane," the woman said.

A female airline employee began taking tickets and the passengers filed onto a small jet.

Eddy found her seat near the back of the plane. *Thank goodness, I got the last aisle seat. There's no way I want to sit by the window in a storm.* She pulled a romance novel out of her purse and began to settle in.

"This is my seat. Move over, missy."

"What?" she looked up from her book. Cigar Man stood in the aisle. "It's *you* again!"

"Shit," he said. "Move over. I'm holding up traffic."

"I will not. This is my assigned seat. You must be in the window seat."

He frowned. "Okay, okay. Move your feet." He squeezed past and wedged himself into the seat next to her.

"And don't bother me," she said pulling down the armrest to mark her territory before reopening her book.

"Don't worry." He crossed his arms and closed his eyes.

The takeoff was bumpy and the captain announced he was keeping the "Fasten Seatbelts" sign on for the duration of the flight. Five minutes later, the plane suddenly lost altitude.

"Oh, shit!" Eddy dropped her book and grabbed for the armrests. Her fingernails dug into Cigar Man's hand.

"Damn, lady!" He jerked his hand back. "Are you trying to kill me? It was just a little air pocket."

She raised her eyelids and stiffened her posture. "I know it was an air pocket. But I wouldn't call it a little one. We must have dropped a couple hundred feet. I don't like sudden drops."

"You probably don't like anything sudden, do you?" He leaned back and closed his eyes.

"What did you mean by that crack?" Her face reddened.

"Umph," he grumbled never opening his eyes.

Before long, a steady *snort—gasp—snort—gasp* erupted from the window seat.

Eddy slammed her book closed and poked Cigar Man in the ribs with her elbow.

"What the hell?" He shook his head and gave her a nasty look.

"You're snoring and I can't read."

"I don't snore."

"Believe me, you snore."

"I don't snore," he declared and tapped the white-haired woman in the seat in front of him on the shoulder. "I don't snore, do I?" he asked gruffly.

"Well … I wouldn't say you snore very loud," the woman said avoiding his glance.

"See," he said turning to Eddy.

"I'm telling you, I can't concentrate with all that noise."

"Live with it." He leaned back and closed his eyes.

"How about I give you a stick of gum? Maybe that will keep you from snoring." She reached under the seat in front of her, pulled out her purse, and rummaged around until she found a package of gum.

"Okay," he muttered. "But I don't like that hot cinnamon stuff."

She handed him a piece of spearmint gum.

I hope he chokes!

Chapter Seven

Quinn watched as a small commuter plane came to a stop in front of the terminal at Four Corners Regional Airport. A motley group of passengers scrambled off the plane and hurried for shelter from the cold wind. The first person through the door was Eddy.

"I thought New Mexico was supposed to be warm. It's freezing out there," she called to Quinn.

"It's November and we're up over 5000 feet." Quinn embraced her friend. "Jeez, you are cold."

"I'm surprised I don't have icicles hanging from my ears," Eddy said and kissed Quinn on the cheek. "We shouldn't be apart this long." Arm in arm the two women strolled the short distance to the baggage claim area.

"Good grief, how many bags did you bring?" Quinn asked after Eddy retrieved three suitcases from the luggage chute and returned for another.

"This is the last one, I promise."

Quinn shook her head. "You're lucky I have an SUV or we'd have to make two trips."

"You know me, always prepared for anything. Ask me about my trip."

"Okay, I'll bite. How was your trip?"

"You're not going to believe this. I called the airline to make my reservations and the dimwit operator connected me with international flights. I said, 'New Mexico is in the United States. You know, wedged between Arizona and Texas.' She still didn't get it, so I had to talk to her supervisor to straighten out the mess."

"I guess a lot of people think New Mexico is part of Mexico."

"Well, they should have paid more attention in geography class. My trip was okay though, except for the delay in Albuquerque. But you know me, I'd make it here come hell or high water. Say, do we need to stop on the way to your place to buy a turkey for tomorrow?" Eddy asked as they headed for the parking lot.

"No. We are having tamales."

"Tamales? Have you gone nuts out here in the middle of nowhere? I brought my special dressing recipe and I'll even volunteer to make it. Are you sure you don't want to change your mind?"

"I appreciate the offer, but I thought it would be fun to celebrate with traditional New Mexico food.

"Whoopee." Eddy pointed her index finger and made circles in the air. "What about the pumpkin pie?" she pouted.

"No pie, we're having bizcochitos," Quinn said, emphasizing the first syllable.

"Bisquick, what?"

"Bizcochitos—New Mexico's official cookie."

"Give me a break. You mean I came all the way out here for Thanksgiving and I have to eat Mexican food, even for dessert." Eddy wrinkled her nose.

"We can have pumpkin pie on Friday and I'll let you make it." Quinn opened the hatch of her Tahoe and began loading luggage.

As if realizing she was getting nowhere, Eddy changed the subject. "How is Rick doing? Does he like living in New York City?"

"He's fine. Still works for the same stock brokerage firm. No sign of a serious girlfriend though."

"Don't rush him. Say, can he get me good theater tickets?"

"For you, he'd flip over backwards."

"You know, when I saw Rick at the funeral, I couldn't get over how much he's starting to look like his father."

"He is, isn't he?" Quinn's thoughts returned to three days after Patrick's funeral.

"I can't believe Dad's gone," Rick said. "Remember that picture of me with the little crappie I caught the first time he took me fishing? According to Dad, it was the biggest fish ever caught in the lake. He could sure tell a good story." Tears welled up in Rick's eyes. He walked across the family room and ran his hand along the bookcase searching for the album containing the photo.

Megan watched him carefully. "You walk just like Dad." Her face turned red and her voice cracked as she continued, "I miss him furiously."

Furious, Quinn told herself. *Furious only begins to describe how I feel about Patrick. Furious the children no longer have a father, furious about his affair, and furious about his death.*

Later in the day, they began the painful process of going through Patrick's closet. They neatly packed all of his clothes into boxes for the Salvation Army.

After the last box was taped shut, Megan announced, "I want to keep Dad's blue golf shirt. Can I?" Tears rolled down her cheeks.

"Of course," Quinn answered.

Megan cut open two boxes and rummaged through them until she found the shirt. "I can still see Dad wearing this—

49

standing in the kitchen on Saturday morning drinking a mug of coffee before he left for the course." She slipped the shirt on. "How do I look?" She did a little twirl.

"Like Dad with long hair and lipstick," Rick said.

Megan gave him a dirty look, but Quinn laughed.

As the children tried on more shirts and teased each other, Quinn took one of Patrick's dress shirts from a box. She placed it on a hanger and hung it by itself in his closet.

Rick held up a brightly colored Hawaiian shirt. "Remember the luau at Dad's office. He sure was funny doing the hula."

The only thing I remember about the luau is Kathy Sullivan's strapless sarong and her bulging boobs, Quinn wanted to say.

"Mom, is it okay if I take Dad's bomber jacket?" Rick asked, "He always looked so sharp when he wore it."

"Sure, take it." Quinn studied her son as he put it on. *He looks like a younger version of Patrick in that jacket. I sure hope he doesn't turn out the same way.*

"Hey, are you in some kind of a trance? Let's get moving," Eddy closed the hatch of the Tahoe.

"What?" Quinn blinked.

"You've been standing there staring off into space."

"Sorry, just thinking." Quinn walked to the front of the car, opened the driver's door, and slid into the seat. "Get in, let's go."

Thanksgiving evening the wind howled around the corners of Uncle Sean's house and the temperature dropped to near freezing. Inside Quinn and Eddy ate dinner in the little dining area of the living room.

"Damn, I need another Margarita, I've got to put out this tamale fire," Eddy fanned her mouth as she spoke.

"I didn't think they'd be this hot." Quinn gulped down the rest of her drink. "I bought them from Maria Quintana, she said they were mild."

"Guess mild is a relative term out here in the Old West."

"The locals say that after the initial burn, the flavor comes through." Quinn took another quick bite of tamale and walked into the kitchen. She returned carrying a large pitcher of margaritas in one hand and a bowl of lime wedges in the other.

"Ah, we can be thankful for simple pleasures," Eddy said taking a piece of lime from the bowl and rubbing it on the rim of her glass. Glancing at the pitcher, she asked, "Are we planning on getting drunk?"

"Well, at least a little tipsy."

After dinner they left the dishes soaking in the sink. Quinn carried another pitcher of margaritas and a plate of bizcochitos to the sofa in the living room.

"Tell me, how are you really coping with this whole Patrick mess?" Eddy asked.

"Some days I don't think about it at all. Other days I find myself crying for no apparent reason. But lately, my mind's been on something else." She curled her feet up under herself and snuggled into the corner of the sofa.

"Ah-ha, that sounds interesting. What's going on?" Eddy sampled a cookie and reached for two more.

"Well, it started out innocently enough and then it grew into an obsession."

"Now, you've got me. What kind of an obsession?" Eddy leaned forward.

Quinn told her about Sam Maxwell. She spared no detail including her physical reaction to the scene in *Inspired by a Kiss*.

"Wow! Now that's what I call a sexy obsession." Eddy rested her head on the back of the sofa.

"But wait until you hear what happened next on the movie set."

"Movie set?"

"He was filming a movie outside of Albuquerque." Quinn recounted the tale of seeing Sam Maxwell and falling into the water trough.

"Oh, no ..." Eddy bent over laughing. "My side is killing me. Oh, oh ..." she roared. "And you got paid two thousand dollars for that ... I can't believe it."

"Believe it," Quinn said.

"I guess it's a done deal then," Eddy said, recovering her wits. "You're a goner when it comes to Sam Maxwell."

"As ridiculous as it sounds, I guess I am." Quinn munched on a cookie and took a sip of her drink. "Did you meet anyone interesting in the Bahamas? You know, a smart, attractive, rich man—one that could pass your two date tryout period."

"Hell, no. Just an obnoxious cigar-smoking jerk." Eddy wrinkled her nose. "I can still smell the disgusting odor of his stogies."

The bizcochitos vanished in an hour but the margaritas flowed until well after midnight.

"Jeez, it's ten o'clock already." Quinn sprang upright in bed. "Yikes! My head feels like it's falling off."

The enticing smell of coffee brewing crept down the hall.

"I can do this. I can get out of this bed and make it to the kitchen." She staggered toward the bedroom door and bumped her head on the doorjamb. "Crap!"

"Girlfriend, is that you making such a racket?" Eddy called from the kitchen.

"Thank goodness for walls," Quinn said leaning against the left side of the hallway outside the kitchen.

"Too much tequila and you pay the price." Eddy looked up from the sink and placed the last clean plate in the dish rack.

"Why are you so cheerful? I think I'm dying." Quinn collapsed onto a kitchen chair and rubbed her head.

"I'm used to having a few drinks. I can pace myself. How long since you've had more than two drinks in one night? And last night doesn't count?"

"You don't want to know."

"I thought so." Eddy placed her hands on her hips. "You've been too good, for too long."

Four cups of coffee and two hours later Quinn peered through the kitchen window. The little courtyard appeared deceptively warm with the noonday's sun shimmering off the ceramic birdbath.

Buzzzz.

"I think your pumpkin pie is ready," Quinn moaned. "And turn that oven alarm off before my head splits."

Eddy tested the pie with a knife blade. "Just right," she said inhaling the pie's fragrance and placing it on a wire rack on the counter. "I can hardly wait for this to cool."

"I've been thinking about this whole Sam Maxwell thing," Quinn said. "You know, I thought seeing him would be the end of my craziness, but it wasn't. It just made matters worse. I can't seem to shake him." She massaged her forehead. "There has to be some reason for all of this, and I'm going to find out what it is."

"And just what do you intend to do?" Eddy raised her right eyebrow.

Quinn stood akimbo. "I'm going on a quest. Do you want to come along?"

"Count me in. When do we start?"

"Soon."

Chapter Eight

Eddy had been gone for a week when the first snow fell. Quinn looked out her bedroom window at the white trees winding their way along the icy water below the bluff.

"I hope it stays like this," she said. "A white Christmas would make things extra special when Rick and Megan get here."

Three days later, Megan called. "I'm so sorry, Mom. I can't come. I used up all my vacation when Dad died. I thought I could take some days off without pay but everyone wants vacation time at Christmas. I'll try to make it out there in January."

The following week, Rick gave her a similar story.

Quinn sat in the recliner next to the fireplace and tried to read the newspaper but could not concentrate.

Our family is always together for the holidays. Why are Rick and Megan abandoning me this year, of all years? I know Christmas will be difficult without their father, but what about me?

She turned to the comics but did not find anything worth laughing about.

Patrick always made such a ritual of decorating the tree and reading The Night Before Christmas. *It didn't matter that the children were grown—they still had to listen to his recitation. Hearing them gripe always made him laugh. Those were happy times. Patrick, why did you have to ruin everything?*

Days passed and still she could not shake her feelings of isolation.

Sensing Quinn's gloom and knowing shopping always cheered her up, Bunny and Linda Lou suggested the three of them go on a shopping trip to Albuquerque. But, it snowed the day they planned to go making the highway too dangerous. They settled for shopping at the mall in Farmington.

"I'm telling you these crowds get bigger every year," Linda Lou said. She set her lunch tray on the small round table where Quinn and Bunny were seated. "I can't believe they refer to this tiny space as a food court."

"Hey, at least they have pepperoni pizza." Quinn devoured a giant slice and did not feel the least bit guilty. "Why are you eating a salad?" she asked looking at Bunny. "It's not like you."

"I've got to slim down before New Year's Eve. I want to start next year out right." Bunny pushed her glasses back but avoided making eye contact.

"Please, you're making me feel guilty." Linda Lou sighed and stared at the extra toppings on her pizza before taking two big bites. "I just need to pick up two more gifts and I'm finished. How about you guys?"

"Actually, I sent Eddy's present home with her. I got her one of the angels she collects. And yesterday I mailed gift cards to Megan and Rick," Quinn said.

"Gift cards? You sent your kids gift cards for Christmas?" Bunny's eyes widened.

"Well, yes." Quinn fidgeted. "I figured if they were too busy to spend Christmas with me, I was too busy to spend hours looking for the right presents for them."

"Wow, that's a cold wind blowing." Linda Lou fluffed her red mane as she spoke.

"Don't get me wrong. I love my children. It's just right now I think they could pay more attention to my feelings."

"After that mess with your husband and his *friend*, I think they could, too." Linda Lou finished her pizza and sipped her soda.

"I'm glad I told you guys about Patrick. I wasn't sure I should air my dirty laundry. But I feel better not having to hide the whole mess."

"That's what friends are for—to understand," Bunny said.

"You know, last year I hinted over and over to Patrick I wanted a carved jade and gold bracelet for Christmas—obviously his mind was someplace else because he bought me a new set of kitchen knives. Boy, if I'd only known, I could have put them to good use."

"I'll say." Linda Lou pretended to sharpen two knife blades by scraping them together.

"Murder and mayhem." Bunny giggled.

"Anyway, if I find a bracelet like that today, I'm buying it for myself. Now, let's get going, we've got shopping to do."

Quinn lingered in bed on Christmas morning looking at the snow crystals glistening on the window pane. Around nine the phone rang. She hurried across the hall to Sean's office and answered it.

"Merry Christmas," Megan said. "Thanks for the gift card. I'm using it to get the new printer I've been wanting for my computer."

Quinn smiled. *Maybe the gift card wasn't such a bad idea despite the reason I bought it.* "I'm glad you like it, honey. I'm just getting up so I haven't opened your present yet, but I know I'll like whatever you sent."

"I hope so. I can't talk long, I'm having a few friends over later today and I have to finish cleaning up and getting things ready. I'm making your special cherry salad. What are your plans for the day?"

"Just a quiet day at home. I'll probably read a book." She scanned Sean's bookcase under the window.

"Sounds boring."

Quinn detected a trace of guilt in Megan's voice. *Well, she should feel guilty.* "Not all of us lead exciting lives, you know," she said.

"You've got to liven up things Mom. Enjoy yourself. I have to go, love you."

Enjoy myself, Megan probably means join a bridge club. She would have a cow if she even got a hint about Sam Maxwell.

Still in her pajamas, Quinn strolled into the kitchen. "I can't face another diet breakfast drink this morning," she muttered. "After all, it's Christmas." She scrambled two eggs, toasted an English muffin, and fixed a cup of hot chocolate.

After breakfast, she studied the miniature Christmas tree in the corner of the living room. It was not anything like the perfectly decorated trees Patrick always insisted on.

What can you expect from a discount special? She sat on the floor next to it and examined her presents.

Megan's gift was tied with a big red bow and seemed to scream, "Open me first!" Quinn untied the ribbon and removed the foil paper. She lifted the lid of the square white box and revealed a blue velvet jewelry pouch. Inside she found a long double-strand of pearls. She put them on over her head, stood, and walked to the mirror hanging over the fireplace.

"Exquisite." She looked at herself as she rolled several pearls between her fingers.

She ambled back to the tree and picked up Rick's present. It was wrapped in paper covered with brown bears in a forest. *Isn't that just like a man?*

Inside the paper was a beautiful jewelry case. She opened it and found a note scrawled in Rick's handwriting. "You are always in my heart," it said. Under the note was a gold bracelet with a heart-shaped charm. Set in the middle of the heart was a diamond.

She held it up to the light and watched it sparkle. Tears streamed down her face.

The children put a lot of thought into choosing special gifts for me this year, and all I sent them were lousy gift cards.

She went to the kitchen to get a tissue and sat at the table wiping her eyes.

I misjudged their intentions and it was your fault, Patrick. If you hadn't cheated on me and then had the audacity to die with that bitch Kathy Sullivan, this wouldn't have happened. I would never have taken out my disappointment at being alone on the children.

A phone call from Rick interrupted her thoughts. "I opened my gift card a couple of days ago and bought a cabinet for my stereo system. I wouldn't have looked at them without the card. Thanks, Mom."

They talked for nearly an hour. A feeling of calm came over her as the conversation ended.

I can face the rest of the day alone. This pity party has to stop.

"What are you doing New Year's Eve?" Linda Lou asked as she and Quinn hit the day after Christmas sale at the Hallmark store.

"I don't have anything planned." Quinn examined a roll of wrapping paper and put it back on the rack.

"I'm going to party at Jake's Place. Why don't you come along? You need to get out and about again."

"I don't want to run the risk of bumping into that louse Davis at Jake's again, so I think I'll call Bunny and see what she's up to," Quinn said.

"Bunny has another date with her mystery man. Besides, Davis isn't that bad."

"As far as I'm concerned, Davis is bad enough," Quinn said.

Linda Lou held up an ornament shaped like a red chile pepper. "I think I'll get a couple of these to tie on presents next year. You know something, sweetie. I'll bet Bunny's mystery man is the reason for her diet." Linda Lou took her ornaments to the cashier and Quinn tagged along.

"She's sure being coy about him. I wish we could figure out who he is," Quinn said. "Anyway, I think I'll just stay home and watch the New Year's Eve celebrations on the television."

Quinn was up early on New Year's Day and decided to call Eddy.

"Do you have any idea what time it is here? It's six in the morning!" Eddy's voice was scratchy and hoarse. "I just got home two hours ago. Give me a break."

"Sorry. It's … well, I've had a lot of time to think and I'm ready to start my quest."

"You mean the Sam Maxwell thing?"

"Yes. This is a new year, a new me and I'm taking action."

"And what is the new you like?" Eddy sounded dubious.

"Just like the old me—but with confidence. I'll be in Los Angeles on the 25th. Can you meet me at the airport?"

"I'll be there ready to rumble."

Chapter Nine

"It feels like a tomb in here," Quinn said entering the house where she spent the last fifteen years of her married life.

"It's just stuffy, I'll open a few windows," Eddy offered and headed for the kitchen.

How weird. I always loved this house, but it doesn't seem like home anymore. Quinn walked into the living room and kicked Patrick's chair out of habit. "I should have gotten rid of this rotten thing before I left," she mumbled.

"You didn't kick that chair again, did you?" Eddy walked around the corner from the kitchen and into the living room. "Remember, the last time you could hardly walk for two days because you hurt your big toe."

"Yes, I kicked it. And I'll keep kicking it as long as it's in my sight. Maybe I should just sell this house and everything in it that reminds me of him." She glared at the chair.

"You better think it over before you do something rash. You might regret it later. It would be a lot easier to just get rid of the chair. It is comfy though," Eddy said flopping onto the cushion.

"Remember, this is the new me. Regret is no longer part of my vocabulary."

"So, Miss Unafraid, how do we start this quest? We aren't going to sit out in front of his house are we?" Eddy asked.

"Don't be silly," Quinn giggled. "Besides, I haven't been able to locate his address.

Eddy raised an eyebrow.

"But I know he has a house out here somewhere and I found a handy bit of information in one of those scandal sheets at the hairdresser." She reached into her purse and pulled out a photo of Sam Maxwell on a tattered piece of newsprint. "The caption says he was sighted jogging near Griffith Park."

"Griffith Park is a big place. Where would we start? Are you sure you want to do this?" Eddy looked skeptical.

"Relax. We're not going to wander aimlessly around Griffith Park. We're going to find the photographer and bribe him for the location."

"If you weren't my best friend, I'd say this is beginning to sound like stalking."

"Don't worry. I'm not planning on breaking into his house, or running his car off the road. I just want a chance to get a better look at him in a nice public place. Maybe I'll wave, or say 'Hi.' He needs to be a real person in my mind, not a fantasy. Then I can get rid of him once and for all."

"Or not," Eddy murmured.

Hercules Ford, the photographer Quinn tracked down, agreed to meet her in the courtyard of Grauman's Chinese Theater at six in the morning.

"I know it's early, but you have to come with me," Quinn begged Eddy. "You never know what kind of pervert you might encounter in Hollywood at that hour. I need backup."

"Do I need a gun?"

"Get serious."

They arrived ten minutes early. Quinn stood in front of the opulent pagoda entrance to the theater. She tilted her head back taking in the façade.

"It's been years since the last time I was here," she told Eddy. "But the theater looks pretty much the same."

The entrance rose ninety feet into the air with three pairs of ornate doors marking the passageway into the theater. Above the doors, carved in stone relief, loomed a thirty-foot dragon. Two huge coral red columns gave support to a bronze roof which displayed the greenish patina of age. In front of each column was an impressive lion-dog, strategically placed to guard the entrance.

"It's still gloriously gaudy, isn't it?" Eddy did the shimmy by one of the lion-dogs.

"Calm down, we don't want to attract too much attention," Quinn said. She surveyed the few tourists undeterred by the early hour.

"Give me a break," Eddy whined. She joined the tourists trying out for size the celebrity footprints and handprints embedded in the concrete slabs covering the area.

"Get over here," Quinn demanded and motioned to Eddy.

Hovering near Burt Reynolds' footprints, the two women scanned the area.

"That must be him over there." Quinn pointed to a mouse of man with a five o'clock shadow and a camera slung around his neck. "He looks haggard, like he's been up all night chasing celebrities."

"He can't be the one. Look at him," Eddy replied.

"Don't underestimate him because of his size. I bet a little guy like that can slip right between the paparazzi thugs and get the good shots."

They approached the man and noticed he was standing in John Wayne's footprints.

"That shrimp can't come close to filling those boots," Eddy whispered.

"Are you Hercules Ford?" Quinn asked.

"Yes. Well ... not really." His eyes darted around the court. "Hercules is my professional name. It helps to insure my ... my privacy."

"I'm Quinn." She held up the picture of Sam. "Can you tell me where in Griffith Park this photo was taken?"

"Where's my two hundred bucks?"

She reached into the pocket of her jeans, pulled out two crisp bills, and held them just out of his reach.

"The secret," he said, "is never giving the right location on your candid shots or some other photog will follow your trail. But seeing as you two ladies aren't my competition, I can tell you the truth. The photo was taken in the San Fernando Valley." He handed Quinn a neatly folded piece of paper.

She gave him a confused stare.

"Open it up, it's a map. You can catch him on that trail every few days when he's in town. He switches around where he jogs to avoid people like me." Hercules snatched the money from Quinn's hand and dashed out of sight.

On the first day of their stakeout, Quinn and Eddy sat on a small stone bench in a grassy area adjacent to the jogging trail.

"This bench is so cold my ass is freezing." Eddy shivered in the early morning air.

"Sorry, but it's important to get out here early if we don't want to miss him." Quinn rubbed her arms to keep warm. "And this location gives us a clear view in both directions."

"Hey, isn't that Hercules Ford behind that big bush about fifteen yards down the trail?" Eddy asked.

"I think you're right."

Hercules occasionally stuck his head out from between the branches and looked in their direction throughout the morning. They flashed him a smile and added a little wave.

"It never hurts to be cordial," Quinn said every time Eddy made a crack about the little man.

A couple of elderly speed walkers journeyed down the path that morning, but no one else appeared. In fact, no one interesting appeared for the next few days.

On the fourth morning, Hercules scampered up the trail.

"I've decided you girls are troopers, so I'm going to give you another place to look in case you miss him here." He handed Quinn a business card for a local nightclub.

Her eyes brightened as she read the name of the place, "The Rainbow Club." *Could this be a sign?*

"It's one of his favorite places." Hercules turned and walked back to his hiding spot.

"How many more mornings do we have to do this?" Eddy asked as the man disappeared.

"Just a few more. If he doesn't show up soon, we'll try the nightclub."

The next morning, Hercules was nowhere in sight.

"Maybe he wised up and is somewhere following a real lead," Eddy said. "On the other hand, you and I are still prime targets for a mugger."

"Get serious. We're perfectly safe."

"Can't we take tomorrow off? I can't stand sitting out here in the cold for one more morning." She rubbed her hands together in a futile attempt to keep them warm. "Besides, didn't God say that on the seventh day we should rest?"

"That's only if the day is Sunday, and tomorrow is Friday."

A tanned, taut-bodied woman with a finely chiseled face strode by like a gazelle.

"You could have given her a run for her money before you married that jerk Patrick," Eddy said.

"After two children and a quarter of a century, I think I'm permanently separated from my flat stomach." Frustrated and freezing Quinn got up from the bench. "Let's go home."

"Wait! That could be him." Eddy pointed up the trail. She pulled a small pair of folding binoculars from the pocket of her sweatpants and took another look. "Yes, I think it *is* him."

"Quick, put plan number one into action." Quinn jumped up from the bench and began jogging in place. "Now remember, don't go too fast. We want him to catch up with us."

"Shit, I think my bones are frozen in place." Eddy struggled to move. "I'll be lucky if I can walk, let alone jog."

The two headed down the trail at a slow trot. After a few paces, Eddy turned and jogged backwards in front of Quinn just as they had planned.

"Is he closing in?" Quinn asked.

"He's about twenty-five yards away. He's picking up speed. I think he's going to pass us."

"Okay, look nonchalant," Quinn demanded. "Now, turn around and drop back beside me."

Eddy slowed, took one more backward step, and tripped over a rock the size of a giant baked potato. Quinn grabbed for Eddy's arm but missed.

"Holy shit!" Eddy screamed as she landed on her rear.

"Can you move?"

"I'm not sure." Eddy looked dazed.

Quinn bent down. "Let me help you." She put her arm under Eddy's shoulder and carefully lifted her to her feet.

"Ow ... ow ... ouch! I think I twisted my ankle when I fell."

"Come on, I'll help you back to the bench."

"What are we going to do now?" Eddy spluttered. "The plan is shot to hell."

"We'll think of something."

"Are you okay, Miss?" a smooth masculine voice crooned. "Let me help you."

Quinn's heart skipped a beat. She turned toward the voice. A familiar face looked down at her. But, it wasn't Sam Maxwell. It was Tom Selleck.

He helped Eddy hobble to the bench and then to her Corvette.

"Guess our days of staking out the jogging trail are over—at least for now," Eddy said as Quinn drove them home.

Quinn's phone woke her in the middle of the night. She rolled over and reached for the receiver on the nightstand.

"Hi, mom." Megan's voice had an unusual timbre.

"What's wrong?" Quinn asked. "You don't sound right."

"Oh, I'm sorry. I didn't mean to scare you."

"Is everything okay?" Quinn asked.

"Everything is great. I just couldn't wait to tell you the news. I'm getting mar-ried," Megan squealed.

In one move Quinn was up and out of her bed. "What did you say?"

"I said—I'm getting married. Perry asked me last night. I'm coming out there next weekend to talk to you about the wedding and Perry's coming with me. Isn't it just wonderful? I know you'll love Perry as much as I do ... I do." She giggled and sang, "*Dum, dum, da-dum.* Sorry, about that. I can't help myself. I'm s-ooo happy." She hung up before Quinn could say anything.

Dazed, Quinn sat on the edge of her bed and studied the phone. *Was that really Megan on the other end of the line? It didn't sound like her at all. Have I been so engrossed in my obsession that I've ignored my own daughter? Crap, I didn't even know she had a boyfriend. I forgot to ask his last name or anything else about him.*

She climbed back under the covers, but tossed and turned.

In the morning, Eddy limped into the kitchen on her sprained ankle carrying a donut pillow for her bruised tailbone.

"I really appreciate you letting me stay here for a few days until I can get around better," she told Quinn.

"No problem." Quinn sat at the counter making a valiant attempt at consuming her diet chocolate breakfast drink.

"What are you doing dressed already?" Eddy asked. "Please don't tell me we're going jogging again."

"I've been up all night. Megan called around midnight. She's getting married."

"Good for her. I was beginning to wonder about that girl, she never seemed to have a boyfriend." Eddy put the coffee on and asked, "Is she pregnant?"

"Good Lord, no. I mean, I don't think so … she's too smart for that. And, what did you mean—you were wondering about her?"

"You know, a beautiful, successful young woman with no man in sight. She did say she was marrying a man, didn't she?" Eddy grinned, opened the cupboard, and retrieved a coffee cup.

"You can't be serious." Quinn thought about the phone conversation. "Well, Megan didn't actually use the word *him*. But she said she is going to marrying Perry. Perry, that's man's name, right?"

Eddy smiled. "Maybe."

"I think I need a real drink," Quinn said and poured her diet breakfast drink down the drain.

The Megan situation weighed on Quinn's mind all day. If anyone knew what Megan was up to it was Rick. She waited until she was sure he would be home from work before phoning him.

"Your sister called last night. She said she's getting married. She is marrying a man isn't she?" Quinn paused but Rick did not take the bait. "And, he isn't a drug dealer or anything like that, is he? Megan acted so strange, I thought she might be high on something. What's going on?"

"Don't panic, Mom. But come to think of it, last time I saw Megan she was pretty high."

Quinn gasped.

"She's been high on love since before dad died, and Perry is definitely a man," Rick laughed.

"This isn't a joking matter young man. Why haven't I heard anything about him?" Her eyes narrowed.

"Megan met him a couple of weeks before the accident. They'd just begun to date seriously when dad died. She didn't think she should be talking about being in love when everyone was so upset."

"So, you've known about this all along, and never said a word to me?"

"I didn't think it was my place. Megan was the one who needed to tell you."

"Is she pregnant?"

"It's not my place to say."

"Rick O'Connor, you can be so aggravating!"

Chapter Ten

Eddy sat on the couch in the den with her legs propped up on the coffee table. Quinn came into the room with a smile plastered across her face.

"What's up?" Eddy asked.

"I just checked my computer and Sam Maxwell is filming at Cal State LA today." Quinn plunked down next to her friend. "I think I'll go take a look."

"So the hunt is back on." Eddy grinned and reached for her purse on the end table.

"Yep."

"Take my car." Eddy dug in her purse and retrieving the keys. "It's been sitting in your garage for a week. The poor thing needs exercise."

Quinn drove across town and pulled Eddy's red Corvette into a corner parking space at Cal State. She opened the door and attempted to get out. The driver's seat was so low and her legs so short she could not get enough leverage to raise her bottom off the seat.

"Crap!" She grabbed the top of the door and gave herself a tug. Emerging from the car she adjusting her skirt and was on her way.

After a short trek across campus, she stood at the corner of a large expanse of grass separating her from the back of the film location. She strained to focus on two men standing just inside a tape barrier.

Her heart fluttered. *The taller one sure looks like Sam.*

She decided to head kitty-cornered across the grassy area. Two steps off the sidewalk the heels of her three-inch pumps sunk into the damp ground.

"Oh, no!" *I knew I shouldn't wear these shoes, but I wanted to look sexy—just in case.*

Twisting her feet, she pulled the heels loose and tottered on the balls of her feet as she continued across the grass.

Gurgling, sputtering, and the distinct smell of water reached her nostrils.

"The sprinklers!"

Frigid water showered her from all directions. She turned and with an awkward duck-like waddle bolted back across the grass on her tiptoes.

"Please God, get me out of here!"

Water soaked her white blouse and strands of wet hair blocked her view as she ran. Her toe hit the edge of the sidewalk stopping her in mid-stride. Her body lurched forward with arms braced for a fall.

"Don't fall. Don't fall!" she prayed.

Staggering forward she regained her equilibrium. She stood straight and pushed the dripping hair from her face. Her blouse was plastered against her skin revealing the outline of her nude lace bra.

One of the men by the tape barrier pointed in her direction.

"Omigod, I hope he can't see through my blouse." She pulled the blouse loose from her skin and shook her skirt. Mustering as much dignity as she could, she marched back to Eddy's car.

Quinn fishtailed the Vette laying rubber as she exiting the parking lot. But, the smoky heat from the tires was no match for her searing hot flash.

"What a disaster!"

"I'll be fine," Eddy told Quinn Thursday evening. "I can sit around at home as easily as I can here. Besides, you'll need some alone time with Megan and Perry when they arrive."

"Are you sure you can drive by yourself? I can take you home," Quinn offered as Eddy sat in her Corvette prepared to leave.

"Thanks, but I can drive without any trouble. I'll call you when I get home." Eddy waved and pulled out of the driveway.

Friday morning flew by. Quinn looked up from scrubbing the kitchen sink and glanced at the digital clock on the microwave—one-thirty. Megan and Perry were due around four o'clock. Her stomach grumbled.

"I'd better not stop to eat if the house is going to look presentable by the time they get here," she mumbled.

The doorbell rang.

"Who can that be?" she asked annoyed by the interruption. *It's too early for Megan. Maybe I won't answer it.*

The bell rang again.

"Okay, okay. I'm coming." She trudged to the front door and glanced in the mirror hanging beside the entrance. A giant brown smudge covered most of her forehead and no hint of makeup was left. Her ratty sweatshirt looked like it was snatched from a rag heap. She removed one cleaning glove and tried to wipe off the smudge.

The lock turned and the door opened almost knocking Quinn down.

"We're here," Megan said giving her mother a warm embrace.

"My gosh! I wasn't expecting you for a few more hours." Quinn tried to pat down her hair. "I look a mess."

"You look great to me," Megan said. "We took an earlier flight, but we can leave and come back at four, if you want."

"Don't be silly. I was just straightening the place a little. I was hoping I'd have time to clean myself up a bit before you arrived. You can't blame a woman for wanting to look presentable when she meets her future son-in-law." She smiled at the dark-haired man standing next to Megan.

"Mom, this is Perry." Megan glowed. She placed her hand in the small of his back and gave him a little nudge.

"It's a pleasure to meet you, Mrs. O'Connor," he said.

Quinn removed her remaining cleaning glove and tossed it onto the small table near the door. She wiped her hand on the side of her sweat pants and offered it to Perry.

"It's so nice to *finally* meet you," she said and looked at Megan out of the corner of her eye.

She gave Perry a quick once-over. He wore thick horn-rimmed glasses and was not much taller than Megan. *A bit on the nerdy side for a criminal defense attorney.* His scuffed white athletic shoes drew her eyes to his enormous feet. *Hmm.*

He held a bouquet of yellow roses in his free hand. "These are for you," he said, handing the flowers to her.

A loud rumble came from Quinn's stomach, but she ignored it thinking no one else could hear the sound.

"How thoughtful, Perry. I'll go put these in a vase." She breathed in their aroma and headed for the kitchen.

"How am I doing?" Perry whispered to Megan as they followed Quinn.

"She's going to love you—just like I do."

Quinn reached into the cupboard and took out the exquisite crystal vase Patrick's grandmother had given her shortly after their marriage.

Just because it came from his side of the family is no reason not to use a perfectly good vase. Maybe I'll give it to Megan after the wedding.

"Look at my ring!" Megan stood next to her mother and held out her hand.

Quinn struggled to keep her mouth from dropping open. Three cushion-cut diamonds rested in an antique platinum setting. The center stone looked at least two carats and the accent stones about a carat each.

"It's absolutely gorgeous," Quinn said looking at Perry.

"It was my grandmother's engagement ring." He smiled.

Quinn's stomach emitted a loud, protracted growl.

Megan arched her eyebrows and tightened her mouth.

Perry grinned. "I think we need to order a pizza."

That evening they made plans for the following day. Quinn and Megan were going shopping for a wedding gown. Perry planned to visit his Uncle Mack and invite him to dinner. Later, they would meet up at Delmonico's. Quinn had been dying for one of their lobsters and having her daughter home provided the perfect excuse to indulge herself.

"How about a friendly game of Scrabble before we call it a day?" Quinn asked.

"Now mother…" Megan started.

Perry interrupted. "Great, I love that game and it's hard to find someone who'll play with me."

The look on Megan's face sent a warning to her mother.

"Fine. I'll get the board," Quinn said.

Perry helped Megan set up the card table and chairs in the living room.

"What was that look about?" he asked.

"There was this game when I was a teenager," she said. "I'd just come home from a party and heard Mom and Eddy laughing in the kitchen. They were drinking wine and playing Scrabble."

"That doesn't sound too bad. Just a couple of friends enjoying themselves," Perry said.

"That's only part of it. Every time Mom played a word Eddy broke into shrieks of laughter. When they noticed me Mom said, 'You're home. How *won-der-ful*. We're having a *won-der-ful* game. Come join us, it would be so *won-der-ful*.' She was drunker than a skunk and mom never gets drunk."

"Maybe she just needed to unwind," Perry said setting up the last folding chair.

"Well, you didn't see the board."

"Oh, come on. It couldn't have been that bad."

"I'm telling you, it was covered with words like *shitfaced,* *dickhead,* and the *F-word.* Then, Eddy played *d-o-u-c-h-e* to which mom promptly added *b-a-g* for a double word score. Those two had lost all sense of decorum, not to mention their spelling skills."

Quinn returned carrying the Scrabble game. "Look Megan, I bought a new one with a turntable."

Megan looked at Perry and sighed.

"Perry you can draw first," Quinn said full of confidence as she set up the board.

They played two games and both were models of propriety. Quinn used her favorite word—*fez.* In a power play, Perry made *zymogram* by attaching all seven of his letters netting bonus points plus a triple word score.

"What does that mean?" Quinn challenged.

"It's a noun, an electrophoretic strip exhibiting the pattern of separated proteins after electrophoresis."

"Oh," she replied as if she understood what he said.

He averaged 400 points per game to Quinn's 250 points and she had a feeling he was not trying too hard.

"How did you become such a good player?" Quinn asked.

"I was on a Scrabble team in college."

"I didn't know there was such a thing as a Scrabble team," Megan said.

Despite getting trounced, by the end of the evening Quinn was enjoying Perry's company.

He has a way of putting people at ease. I can see how Megan fell in love with him.

Megan began wiggling into her fifth wedding gown of the morning.

"Mom, I'm stuck," she squealed from beneath layers of satin and organza.

Quinn could see her daughter's engagement ring sparkle as her hand reached out from the top of the designer wedding gown.

"Did you unzip it all the way?"

"I think so, but can you check it for me? I'm suffocating in here."

"It's only halfway down and I think it's stuck," Quinn said fiddling with the zipper.

A musical ringtone erupted from the corner of the over-sized dressing room. "That's Perry calling. Can you get my cell, it's in my purse?"

Quinn retrieved the tiny phone and glanced at Megan. "Ah, where do you want it?"

"Slip it up under the dress. No, no, that won't work. My head's stuck. You'll have to answer it."

Quinn flipped open the phone. "Perry, can you hold for a minute?" She set the phone on the dressing room chair and walked back to Megan. One swift jerk on the zipper and it slid all the way down releasing Megan from her bridal prison.

Megan shuffled to the chair with the dress hanging around her waist. She picked up the phone. "Hi, honey," she cooed. "Oh, I'm sorry. Yes, we'll meet you there around six. I love you, bye."

"What's up?" Quinn asked.

"Perry says his Uncle Mack won't be able to join us for dinner because he has to catch an early evening flight to New York on business."

"What kind of business is he in?"

"I don't know. But he's very rich. Perry says in addition to his house in Beverly Hills he has a ranch in Hawaii, and an apartment in New York."

"Wow, it must be nice to have an uncle like that."

"Oh, he isn't really Perry's uncle. He's his godfather—his father's best friend from college. But even though he isn't flesh and blood, he's Perry's favorite uncle. He doesn't have any children of his own so he takes Perry skiing and fishing a lot. When he was a teenager, Perry used to spend his summers working on Uncle Mack's ranch on the Big Island."

"He sounds like a nice man."

"Yeah, I guess so. I've never met him."

Quinn looked at the rumpled mass surrounding Megan's waist. "Now, pull that top up and let's see how this dress looks."

Megan and Quinn were singing *Going to the Chapel* as they made the turn onto LaCienaga Boulevard in Beverly Hills and headed for Delmonico's. Perry was waiting for them in the parking lot.

"How was your day, sweetheart?" he asked slipping his arm around Megan's waist as they walked to the entrance.

"I found the perfect wedding dress," she said full of excitement. "Of course, I can't tell you anything about it. And, we found some beautiful pink dresses for the bridesmaids. I just love pink in the summertime."

"So do I," he said and pulled her tighter.

Quinn found it remarkable how Perry could bring out the giddy side of serious Megan.

"I'm sorry you won't get a chance to meet my uncle today," Perry said to Quinn. "I think you'd like him." He gave Megan a quick peck on the cheek. "He's offered us the ranch for our honeymoon. What do you think, sweetheart? Are you up to some hula time?"

Megan and Perry had to return to Pennsylvania Sunday afternoon, so the morning was busy. From Megan's stack of sample wedding invitations they decided on a simple style printed on recycled paper. Megan and Perry agreed to reserve a church in Philadelphia and pick out a location for the reception.

They were to consult with Quinn over the phone about the details. Perry called his uncle in New York and accepted the honeymoon offer.

"Mom, don't forget you promised to be in Philly a month before the wedding to help with all of the last minute stuff," Megan said.

Quinn took Megan into the kitchen. "Megan, one thing has been bothering me about all of this. Everything has been so fast. Are you pregnant?"

Megan laughed. "Do you think I'd wait until summer to get married, if I was?"

"You can never tell with all these celebrities getting married when they are seven or eight months pregnant. Some of them even wait until after their babies are born."

"Well, you never know." Megan smiled. "Maybe you'll have a grandchild waiting for you when you get to Philly."

After Megan and Perry left, Quinn sat at the kitchen table munching on a raw carrot. She missed them already.

He's such a nice young man. But Megan didn't answer my question, did she?

Chapter Eleven

The expansive kitchen windows of Eddy's cliff-top home provided a great view of the Pacific Ocean. Perched on a Lucite barstool next to the granite breakfast counter, Quinn gazed at the aquamarine waves lapping the shore below.

"It's so peaceful here," she said, turning to watch Eddy fix chicken salad for lunch.

"Except when the seagulls are on a rampage." Eddy tossed chopped, hard-boiled eggs into the bowl with the diced chicken.

"Speaking of rampages—Megan didn't go on one while she was here because she never found out about Sam Maxwell. I didn't mention him once," Quinn said.

"Good for you. She probably wouldn't have understood." Eddy walked to the fridge and took out the mayonnaise.

"Are you kidding? She'd have had me committed and maybe you, too." Quinn took two plates from the cupboard and placed them on the kitchen table. "But you know, it doesn't matter whether I talk about him or not—I keep thinking about him." She paused for a minute. "How's your ankle doing?"

"As good as new, but my ass still hurts if I'm not careful when I sit down." Eddy placed the salad on the table and walked to the drawer next to the stove to get the silverware.

"Are you up to dancing?" Quinn asked, taking a seat.

Eddy sat across from her. "I'm up for whatever you want."

"Then I'm thinking we ought to check out that nightclub—the one on the card Hercules gave me."

"When do you want to go?"

Quinn leaned forward and smiled. "How about tonight?"

"Are you sure you want to do this?"

"I have this feeling inside that's driving me crazy. Before I go back to New Mexico, I need to try to see him one more time."

"You're going back? I was hoping you'd come home to stay." Eddy passed her the bowl of salad.

"I'm not sure I'll ever live here again. My house feels so strange." Quinn put a large dollop of the chicken mixture on her plate and handed the bowl to Eddy. "Everywhere I look there's something that reminds me of Patrick. Then I think about him with Kathy. The next thing I know, I'm kicking his chair, or breaking down and crying my eyes out. That's no way to live."

"I guess I understand. I had a hard time in this house for months after Tom died. And there wasn't another woman in the picture." She put some chicken salad on her plate and took a bite. "Tonight is Wednesday—shouldn't we wait until the weekend to go to the club?"

"I've heard celebrities go out on Wednesday nights. You know, to avoid all the regular people. So, tonight might be perfect."

"What about his bodyguard?" Eddy asked. "Nowadays, most famous people have them."

"Jeez, I didn't think about that. I've never seen him at any of those red carpet events on television. In fact, I don't remember ever seeing him until I watched that darn movie. He's supposed to be famous, but I don't think he's one of those A-list celebrities with a bodyguard."

"Okay then, wear that low-cut blue dress you bought last week. If Sam's there, you'll catch his eye in that sexy little number." Eddy shimmied provocatively.

Just outside Westwood's city limits, Eddy pulled her red Corvette to a stop in front of The Rainbow Club. The two women stepped out as gracefully as possible and headed for the entrance. Eddy tossed her keys to a parking valet who sped off in the car.

"Hi, girls. I figured you'd show up sooner or later."

Quinn and Eddy turned to see Hercules Ford lurking near the side of the building.

"Is he here?" Quinn asked.

"I haven't seen him and I've been here since eight. Wednesday's are always a good bet though. He usually doesn't show up until about now. He'll probably be alone, but I have to keep watching in case he shows up with a new squeeze. One good picture will pay my rent for a month."

Quinn looked at Eddy and then back to Hercules. "Does he have a bodyguard?"

"Not usually," the little man replied. "He's been a star for years. Even though people are interested in what he's up to, most of the time he doesn't get hassled."

"Let's go inside," Eddy said. "It's too chilly in these dresses to stand around talking all night."

"I wish I could join you, but I'm banned from the place. Good hunting." Hercules gave them a little salute and leaned back against the building.

Signed photos of famous faces lined the walls of the nightspot. They reminded Eddy of the caricatures decorating Sardi's in New York. Even the name of the place was reminiscent of New York City.

"This isn't a hot spot for the younger set," Eddy told Quinn as they surveyed the middle-aged patrons.

"I'd say from the size of women's diamonds and the cut of the men's suits, this might be a good hunting ground for a well-to-do husband." Quinn gently poked Eddy in the ribs. "You might want to remember this place."

"Men may be my passion, but I don't need one to support me," Eddy said.

"With the millions Tom left you, I guess you only need a man now—when you need a man.

"You've got it," Eddy said. "But there are some good-looking men in here."

"Let's find a place to sit where we can see everyone," Quinn said and started toward the back of the club.

Eddy was sure the "sign thing" had gone off in Quinn's head when she first saw the club's business card. *She probably thinks there's some cosmic significance to the name of this place. After all, she saw a rainbow right after the first time she laid eyes on Sam Maxwell.*

Eddy didn't believe in signs, but she knew Quinn was a firm believer. It all started when they were teenagers. Jimmy Drexler's car had a flat tire in front of Quinn's house and a week later he asked her out on a date. Quinn said the fact that the flat happened where it did was a sign of things to come.

Why did I let myself get sucked into another Sam escapade? Because I owe Quinn big time—that's why. She was there for me during my divorces and when Tom died. And she'll be there the next time I need her. Standing by her tonight is least I can do.

"The jazz is great, isn't it?" Quinn found a booth in the back with a clear view of the entrance.

"Yeah, that Mockingbird Trio is a little gem." Eddy said. "The pianist can improvise *It Don't Mean a Thing* with the best of them."

Two margaritas and one piña colada later there was still no sign of Sam.

Eddy nudged Quinn. "See the man facing the bar? The one who keeps looking at his watch."

"The guy with the dark hair?"

"That's the one. I'm sure I know him from somewhere."

"You know plenty of men from somewhere."

Eddy tried to get a good view of the man's face, but the bar was too far away. "Oh, well. I guess it's not important."

"I understand why Sam loves this place," Quinn said running her fingers over the supple leather upholstery of their booth.

"Yeah," Eddy said but she was getting restless. "Well, if we're going to stay, I'm requesting *Georgia on My Mind.*" She stood and adjusted her tangerine slip dress. Her long coral earrings swayed as she traipsed across the room.

The dark-haired man still stood at the bar, but it was the hunky bartender who caught Eddy's attention as she approached.

He's too young for me. But there isn't any harm in appreciating God's masterpieces.

"Would you like to use our phone, Mr. Winter?" the bartender asked the dark-haired man.

"Thanks, but I'll just get a table and wait a while longer." He turned and walked toward the dance floor.

Eddy's mouth went agape when she saw his face.

Mr. Winter is Cigar Man! No wonder he looked familiar. She regained her composure and skulked back to the booth hoping he had not noticed her.

"It's him!" she told Quinn as she eased herself into the booth. "It's that uncouth fathead from the Bahamas."

"He doesn't look uncouth to me. Actually, he doesn't look half-bad."

"Well, I can't stand the man. Look, he's checking his watch again. I'll bet he's been stood up, it would serve him right." Eddy smiled.

Mr. Winter looked up from his diamond studded Rolex and glanced across the room. He sipped his martini and nodded at the piano player who began playing *Georgia on My Mind.* Three tunes later, he looked at his Rolex again.

"What do you think is going on with him?" Eddy asked. "I'll bet he's up to no good." She scooted out of the booth "And I'm going to find out what it is."

"Wait. What are you going to do?"

"Just a little reconnaissance." Eddy walked over to the band, found a table close to Mr. Winter, and sat with her back toward him.

A cocktail waitress showing considerable cleavage and with long legs jetting out from under her short skirt carried a phone to him. "Sir, a call for you."

Eddy could not hear the caller but listened intently to Mr. Winter.

"I left my cell at home so we wouldn't be disturbed. Where the hell are you?" He paused for a few moments. "Shit. I'll be right there." He hung up the phone and headed for the exit.

Eddy returned to the booth. "Boy, it sounded like some woman has him whipped."

"You should have seen the look on his face when he hung up the phone," Quinn added. "Maybe we should go, too. I don't think Sam's going to show up tonight."

"First, let's toast the woman who put Cigar Man in his place." Eddy held her glass high and then downed the rest of her piña colada before following Quinn out of the nightclub.

Quinn looked around as they stepped into the night air. "I don't see Hercules."

"Ah, the little mouse. He's probably running up the trail of another big cheese by now," Eddy said and motioned for the valet to bring her car around.

The two women jumped into the Corvette and zoomed off into the night.

"These are absolutely lovely," Quinn told the deliveryman as he handed her a tall vase containing a dozen perfect red roses. She walked into the living room and placed the bouquet on the coffee table.

Eddy was sitting in Patrick's chair. "Who are they from?"

"Sam Maxwell, of course." Quinn smiled a wicked smile. "Who do you think they're from?" She sat on the couch and admired the flowers. "Rick sent them."

"Oh, tomorrow is Valentine's Day, isn't it?" Eddy gave a mock smile of surprise.

"Don't act like you forgot. You never forget Valentine's Day."

"How do you expect me to remember? No one sent me roses." Eddy frowned and pretended to sniffle.

"I'm sure Rick sent them because he remembered his dad always sent me a dozen roses on Valentine's Day."

"Every year?"

"He never missed a year even when he was out of town. Last year he was in Seattle and the roses arrived right on schedule." She leaned back into the couch and cracked her knuckles. "But he was probably somewhere else with Kathy Sullivan," disgust mixed with hurt echoed in her voice.

"Maybe he really was in Seattle."

"Don't stick up for him," Quinn snapped. "I can't believe a word he ever said to me anymore. He could have been lying the whole time we were married for all I know." Anger gripped her and she remembered a day about a month after his death.

"Liar!" she yelled running up the stairs to her bedroom.

She yanked Patrick's remaining shirt from the closet. Suddenly, she knew she had saved the shirt for a time like this. With newfound strength, she ripped it in two just like she wanted to rip Patrick in two. She opened the nightstand drawer and grabbed the scissors from inside. With fire in her eyes, she snipped each portion of the shirt into tiny bits and threw them in the wastebasket.

"You'll never lie to me again," she shouted.

Eddy looked at Quinn's furrowed brows. "Don't dwell on Patrick. It's Valentine's Day tomorrow—enjoy the roses."

Chapter Twelve

A letter from Robert Repenski put a crimp in Quinn's plans to return to New Mexico.

"Repenski, Patrick, and Uncle Sean were old fishing buddies," Quinn told Eddy, "but the letter had nothing to do with fishing. Repenski is also Uncle Sean's lawyer. So, I was a bit on edge when the letter arrived yesterday. It says my uncle passed away and requests that I be in Chicago for the reading of his will."

"I'm so sorry. I know how much your uncle meant to you," Eddy said, sipping iced tea in Quinn's kitchen.

"His death wasn't entirely unexpected. He'd been in bad health for the last few years. When I called Repenski to see if I could get out of going, he told me Sean slipped away in his sleep after a week of medical crises." Quinn shivered at the thought of her dear uncle dying without family near him.

"Did he say why you need to be there?"

"He said Uncle Sean had specifically requested that I be there. I told him I really didn't want to see his cold lifeless body and I'd rather remember him alive, but Repenski was adamant. He repeated my uncle's desire that I be there for both the funeral and the reading of the will. Repenski said my mother's sisters would need me there for support."

"I can understand why you need to go. When are you leaving?"

"Tomorrow."

Quinn stared out the window of the plane. The stark iceberg-like clouds on the horizon echoed the arctic emptiness she felt at the loss of her uncle.

She thought about the special relationship Uncle Sean and Patrick had developed over the years. *If Patrick were alive, he would have rushed to his side as the end grew near.* She smiled for a moment. *Patrick did have some good qualities.*

Bob Repenski was waiting for her at the baggage terminal. Years had passed since she'd last seen him, but Quinn recognized him immediately. He still had the gaunt body of a runner and the angular features of his face remained pretty much the same.

He lifted her suitcase from the luggage carousel, extended the handle and rolled it behind him as they walked the short distance to a waiting limousine.

"I'm sorry we have to meet again under such sad circumstances," he said and assisted her into the car.

"Uncle Sean was a wonderful person," Quinn's voice cracked as she continued, "I'm going to miss him terribly."

"Me, too. We were friends for over fifty years." He walked around to the other side of the limo and climbed inside. "I was there that night ... the night he died. He was in good spirits and seemed to be improving." His tone lowered, "If I'd thought there was any chance he wouldn't make it through the night, I would never have left."

"I know," she said touching his hand.

They sat in silence as the driver wound his way through the streets of Chicago. Quinn looked out the tinted window and pretended to take in the sights. Her mind was full of memories of her uncle.

Repenski broke the silence. "Sean was emphatic about wanting a simple graveside service. All the weeping and eulogizing that takes place in churches and funeral homes, wasn't his style."

"That sounds like him."

"I was sorry to hear about Patrick's death. We had great times fishing down on the San Juan."

"It doesn't seem possible, but he's been gone almost a year now," she said.

"Sean loved that man like a son. He was crushed when he was too ill to attend his funeral."

"He sent his regards and the kids and I knew we were in his thoughts. It was generous of him to offer me the use of his vacation home, so I could get away for a while." After a short pause she asked, "Will there be a viewing tonight?"

"Sean didn't want one. He said it was too morbid. You know, he didn't let anyone except me visit him during the last two months. He said he looked like death warmed over and didn't want to scare people. Actually, I think he didn't want a viewing because he was too vain to have friends see him in his deteriorated condition."

Quinn smiled. "You're probably right about that. Even in old age, he was a head-turner. I don't remember ever seeing him when he wasn't fastidiously dressed and groomed. In fact, I always had a hard time imagining him as the expert fly-fisherman Patrick bragged about."

"A lot of people didn't believe he spent his free time fishing. I guess they couldn't imagine him mucking around in the mud. But he loved the challenge."

"Is the service still at nine?" she asked as they approached her hotel.

"It's been moved to ten o'clock so the old folks, like me, will have time to get there. The reading of the will is planned for two in the afternoon at Sean's house. I've made sure you'll have a driver at your disposal," he said.

The next morning was overcast adding to Quinn's gloomy mood. Like her uncle, she hated funerals. A limo was waiting outside her hotel. She rode the short distance to the cemetery feeling depressed. The last funeral she had attended was Patrick's.

Facing his friends was the most embarrassing experience of my life. The men and especially the women seemed genuine in their condolences but there was pity in their eyes—pity for a woman scorned. If only I could have told them how I really felt. Pity smitty! The real pity was that I didn't find out sooner and kill him myself.

The words she spoke over Patrick's grave a week after his funeral came back to her. *How could you do this to your family? How could you have made a mockery of everything I believed?* She remembered kicking dirt on his grave. *I will never forgive you, you bastard!*

The sky had cleared by the time the limousine pulled through the cemetery gates and stopped near the grave site. Quinn walked the short distance to a large canopy set up in front of the coffin. The sun reflected off the bronze trim of the highly polished oak casket that rested above the open grave. The chairs beneath the canopy were almost full. She surveyed the mourners looking for familiar faces. Her aunts, Martha and Sally, were seated in the front row.

"Quinn dear, we're over here," Aunt Martha called and waved for her to join them.

Aunt Martha was a woman with a sweet face, substantial bulk, and stood almost six feet tall. Fortunately, the chairs were not pushed too close together because Martha's enormous bottom always flapped over the edges of folding chairs. Aunt Sally, on the other hand, was like a tiny sparrow—delicate and soft spoken. Neither one looked anything like Quinn's mother, Betty. In her prime, Betty was frequently compared to former Miss America Bess Myerson. Yet, there was a sameness about the three sisters—something comforting.

Quinn recalled the story of how her grandfather's brother, Jack Delaney, used to razz her grandmother about the three girls.

"If I didn't know you were such a tight-assed churchgoer, I'd swear you slept with three different men," Jack would say. Then he would add, "Sean and Betty look so much like their father they must be the only true Delaneys."

Grandma Delaney would swing her rolling pin at him and yell, "Well, Jack, you'll have to admit that all my children have a *gentle temper*, just like their mother," as she chased him around the house.

These days it seemed to Quinn like she was exhibiting more and more of her grandmother's temperament.

"Did you notice that the two hussies are here?" Aunt Martha whispered as Quinn sat next to her.

"I can't believe they had the nerve to show up," Aunt Sally added pursing her lips.

Quinn had spotted Sean's two longtime paramours, Lizzy and Amanda, among the throng of mourners when she arrived.

"They look pretty broken up," Quinn said.

"*Humph.*" Martha crossed her arms. "Those black dresses and designer sunglass make me sick. And all that loud sobbing—the only thing they're sobbing about is that he didn't die sooner so they could get their hands on his money."

"You think he left them money?" Quinn asked.

"Well, I'm sure that's what they think."

"Hush, the service is starting," Aunt Sally said and folded her hands.

According to Sean's wishes, the memorial service was short and not overly sentimental. But, as Aunt Sally remarked, "The flowers were lovely."

A few minutes before two o'clock, Quinn filed into Uncle Sean's den along with six other people—Repenski, Martha, Sally, her uncle's two lady friends, and a man she didn't recognize.

"Quinn dear, I can't tell you how much Sally and I appreciate you being here," Aunt Martha said. She put her arm around Quinn and gave her a hug.

"Betty would be pleased, it's almost like she's still here," Sally said with a tear in her eye.

"Please be seated ladies and gentleman," Repenski announced. "Sean Delaney left a video edition of his will, explaining his bequests." He pushed a button on the wall and the rich, oak paneling slid to the left revealing a huge television. "Are we ready?" He looked around the room. "Okay, let's begin." He started the recording.

Uncle Sean appeared on the screen looking remarkably fit considering his weakened health. He began with the required legal language and then got to the specifics. After expressing his love for his sisters, Sean bequeathed each of them a million dollars.

Martha and Sally gasped.

He moved on to his fiftyish lady friends. "I love you both. You have given me years of immense physical pleasure." He sighed, as if remembering.

Quinn recognized the naughty twinkle in Sean's eyes. *How much more explicit is he going to get?*

Her elderly aunts blushed and shifted uneasily in their chairs.

"Lizzy, my dear, what can I say? You have the most exquisite breasts I have ever seen."

Aunt Martha choked and crossed her arms.

Aunt Sally gulped for air and pursed her lips.

Sean continued, "But Amanda has always been my favorite."

Lizzy's mouth dropped open and her eyes shot daggers at Amanda who smiled smugly.

"So, Lizzy my dear, I am leaving you five hundred thousand dollars. That's a quarter of a million dollars for each breast," he chuckled. "I hope you will store away the money for your future."

"Amanda, my love, I leave you one million dollars."

"Bitch!" Lizzy yelled. She jumped from her chair and ran toward Amanda. "You conniving slut, I deserve as much as you do!"

"Obviously, you don't," Amanda shot back.

Repenski clicked off the video and together with the unfamiliar man dashed for the two women. Lizzy grabbed Amanda by the hair, pulled her from the chair, and pushed her to the floor. Amanda stuck her leg out and tripped Lizzy who fell with a thud. Repenski and the other man each grabbed a woman around her waist and dragged them from the room.

"Well, I never ..." Aunt Martha began.

"... have seen such a sight," Aunt Sally finished.

Quinn was speechless.

A few minutes later Repenski, minus the other man, returned to the room. "Sean anticipated there might be trouble. That's why Mr. Armstrong was here for security. Shall we continue?"

The women nodded in agreement. Repenski restarted the video.

"Quinn, my precious niece, you and your departed Patrick were always special to me. As a token of my esteem, I leave you the house on the San Juan River that holds so many happy memories for me. In addition, I leave you five hundred thousand dollars for its upkeep."

Quinn looked at the lawyer in disbelief. Repenski winked at her.

The video ended with a list of charities that were to receive the balance of the estate.

"This has certainly been some day," Aunt Sally said as she stiffly rose from her chair. "Who would have guessed Sean had stashed away so much money?"

"More excitement than I've seen in years," Aunt Martha added. "Do you suppose those two hussies are still brawling out in the hall?"

Chapter Thirteen

Back in New Mexico, Quinn returned to her usual routine. Every morning she hiked the trail down to the river and back. This morning she stood beside the muddy bank and looked up at her house on the bluff.

It really is my house.

From a distance it looked different—more inviting. Perhaps it was because she would never have to leave again. She filled her lungs with the high desert's invigorating air, sat on a boulder, and contemplated the blue vault of heaven.

Her daily hikes provided the perfect chance to mull over her problems with a clear head. Today she weighed the pluses and minuses of selling her house in California.

I don't owe any money on it, thanks to mortgage insurance. But it seems a waste to keep such a big house when it's empty most of the time. Besides, every time I step inside the place the wounds of Patrick's cheating reopen. It makes sense to sell, especially now that I have this house.

She started back up the trail. About halfway home, a small cotton-tailed rabbit scurried across the path in front of her.

You can't see that at home ... home. She sighed. *No, I can't sell the house. It's where the children grew up—it holds happy memories too. But, I'm sure as shootin' getting rid of that damned chair.*

Angry squawks from a gaggle of Canada geese interrupted Quinn's reading on the deck that afternoon.

"Now, what?" She got up from her chair and walked to the railing. The geese were fussing over something by the edge of the water but she could not make out what it was. The creatures reminded her of Lizzie and Amanda squabbling over Uncle Sean's estate.

For him to keep those two harpies around so long, they must have been fabulous in bed. After all, with his money he could have hired a couple of young things instead of messing around with two women past their prime.

Lizzie's breasts obviously sent him into a sweat. Why else would he have left her a half million dollars for their care? With her demeanor, she'd make a superb dominatrix. I wonder if Uncle Sean had a kinky side.

Amanda's alabaster skin is perfect for diamonds. Maybe he adorned her with jewels when they made love.

Out of nowhere Uncle Sean's face appeared before Quinn. His eyes twinkled and he laughed at the bizarre scenarios in her mind.

"Jeez." A shiver ran through her body. "I've got to stop thinking about this stuff. It doesn't matter what his sexual tastes were. The real point is he didn't throw his women overboard when they got older. In fact, he seemed to find them as attractive as ever."

She sauntered into the house, fixed half a tuna salad sandwich, and grabbed a diet root beer from the bottom shelf of the fridge. Two bites into her snack she looked at the calendar hanging nearby. Saturday would be April 13th—the first anniversary of Patrick's death.

"Why did you do it?" she said. "It's not like I let myself go. Sure, I gained a few pounds in twenty-six years, but so did you." She got madder with each bite of her sandwich. "How could you just throw our marriage away on that little tramp? You had no reason to cheat on me!"

She paced the kitchen floor. Taking a red marker from the junk drawer she walked to the calendar and placed a giant "X" on April 13th.

"I'm not taking this shit any longer. This will be my red-letter day. I'm going to celebrate your death, you two-timing bastard. I'll show cleavage, dance like a fool, and drink margaritas on Saturday night!"

Thursday Quinn was on the treadmill at the fitness center gearing up for her big night. Sweat dripped off the back of her hairline and trickled down between her shoulder blades soaking her shirt.

Time to cool off.

She strolled over to the break area and spied Bunny and Linda Lou huddled deep in conversation.

"What's up?" she asked settling into a chair at their table.

"Bunny's thinking about changing her hairdo. What do you think?" Linda Lou asked.

Quinn studied her friend's antique beehive and tried to find a diplomatic way of agreeing. "Well, I think we all need a change every now and then." She thought for a moment. "In fact, I'm making a change myself. Instead of staying home this weekend, I'm going to Jake's on Saturday night."

Bunny looked shocked. "You're kidding. What brought this on—nothing good on satellite?" She grinned and leaned forward. "I don't want to miss a word of this."

"I'm celebrating the anniversary of Patrick's death."

"Great. It's about time you got that monkey off your back." Linda Lou straightened in her chair. "Good riddance." She folded her arms across her chest.

"I think it's wonderful that you're ready to move on," Bunny said.

"I bought myself a sexy blouse, a pushup bra, and a pair of tight jeans." Quinn's voice conveyed a newfound confidence.

"I've got to see this. Need company Saturday night?" Linda Lou asked.

"Actually, I was going to invite both of you to come along. Dinner will be my treat. How about it?"

"I can come for dinner. But, I have a date later," Bunny said adjusting her glasses.

"Another date? Who is this guy?" Linda Lou prodded.

"Just someone who makes me feel wonderful." Bunny beamed and turned a little red.

"Well, I'll be there," Linda Lou said, "and I can stay the whole evening."

Quinn looked in the bedroom mirror at her scanty garnet blouse and matching pushup bra peeking out at the neckline.

"Not bad for almost fifty." She placed a teardrop diamond pendant at the rise of her breasts to accent her cleavage. Her dark denim jeans, high-heeled garnet sandals, and gold chandelier earrings completed her new look. "This ought to do the trick, I'll be dancing tonight."

At seven sharp, Quinn sat in a corner booth at Jake's waiting for her friends. Bunny and Linda Lou arrived ten minutes later.

"Sorry, we're late ... " Linda Lou stopped mid-sentence and looked Quinn up and down. "What happened to you?"

"I don't believe my eyes," Bunny chimed in and adjusted her glasses.

"I wouldn't do it. I was all dressed up, cleavage bursting out all over the place and I just couldn't do it." Quinn sat primly attired in black slacks and a white blouse. Only the chandelier earrings hinted at her former outfit. "I felt so ... so uncomfortable with how I looked."

"Well, at least you're here. Let's order. I'm having the *chicken* enchiladas," Bunny said directing her glance at Quinn.

"Guess I deserved that. I'll have some too." Quinn looked at the menu printed on the tablecloth. "And a diet coke."

"Better change that to a margarita," Linda Lou said raising her eyebrows. "You need to loosen up, sweetie."

After dinner Quinn scanned the bar for Davis. He was nowhere in sight. She breathed a sigh of relief.

"The pickings are slim tonight," Linda Lou said. "Wonder where everyone is?"

"Where's the waitress? I need another margarita," Quinn said.

True to her word Bunny left at eight.

The band started playing and a group of rowdy young partygoers arrived. They took a booth two down from Quinn and Linda Lou.

"This place doesn't usually attract the younger crowd. I wonder where they came from." Linda Lou fluffed her hair, eyeballed the group, and frowned.

"They're just having fun. I wouldn't worry about them," Quinn said.

A few minutes later there was an abrupt change in mood in the nearby booth. A strapping young man in a black AC/DC T-shirt jumped out of the booth and jerked a petite blonde after him. He hustling her toward the door.

"What the hell were you doing flirting with Greg?" the man yelled.

Quinn looked at Linda Lou. "Maybe that's what I should have done the first time I saw Patrick smile at that bitch Kathy."

"Maybe so, but it's not your style."

Quinn and Linda Lou listened to the band and nursed a few more drinks before leaving at eleven.

"Some celebration," Quinn groaned that night as she slipped into her nightgown. "No cleavage—no dancing—three margaritas and one Shirley Temple. Pitiful!"

Sunday morning Quinn lumbered around the house unable to get in the groove to do much of anything. She picked up the unworn garnet blouse from the bedroom floor, placed it on a hanger and hung it in the closet.

Why did I let myself ruin the celebration of Patrick's death? She sighed in disgust. "Sam will cheer me up," she murmured and schlepped down the hall to the living room.

She searched for *Inspired by a Kiss* in the stack of DVDs on the fireplace but it wasn't there. She checked the bookcase and under the cushions on the couch. The movie seemed to have vanished. Frustrated she sank down on the couch, stretched out and dozed off.

A few minutes later, the telephone jolted her awake. She grumbled at the interruption of her Sam Maxwell dream.

Why isn't there a phone next to the couch?

On the second ring she threw her leg over the edge of the couch and smashed her knee into the coffee table.

"Crap!" Her knee screamed in pain. She limped toward the kitchen. "This better be important," she whined.

The phone rang three more times before Quinn got to the receiver.

"Oh, I'm so glad you're home! I need to come over," Linda Lou said in a frenzy. "It's an emergency!"

"Well, I guess, sure ..."

"Great. I'm on my way."

Quinn stood dumbfounded as the receiver went dead.

The sound of tires on her gravel driveway and the thud of her trash can sent Quinn rushing into the courtyard. She peered over the gate at the upended can in front of Linda Lou's Cadillac.

A fuzzy pink slipper attached to a bare skinny leg kicked open the driver's door. Linda Lou sprang from the car in a pink bathrobe with a matching pink towel wrapped around her head. On her arm she carried a large pink tote decorated with a black sequined cat. The puff of pink dashed across the driveway toward the courtyard.

Quinn opened the gate and Linda Lou scrambled inside. Her face was flushed and her eyes looked ready to pop out of their sockets.

"Sorry, about the trash can. But you're not going to believe what happened." She panted and held her chest. "You know, I'm starting that part-time ..." she gasped for air, "job at Hugo Smithpepper's law office tomorrow?"

"Yes."

"Well, look at this!" She pulled the towel off her head revealing a mass of flaming orange hair.

"Whoa, girl! You've been watching too many *I Love Lucy* reruns."

"This is serious. I looked in the mirror this morning and all I could see were my gray roots staring back at me. So, I decided to fix them myself. You know, because it's Sunday and all. Now look at the mess I'm in!" She started to bawl.

Quinn gave her a hug. "Come on, let's go into the house. Did you call Curly Cuts? Maybe Marge can come in special to fix your hair."

"I tried, but all I got was her answering machine saying she'd be out of town until next Saturday." Linda Lou's shoulders heaved and tears ran down her cheeks. She threw her tote on the kitchen table and slumped into one of the chairs.

"So, what are you going to do?" Quinn tried not to stare at Linda Lou's hair.

"Oh, this is a terrible mess. If I show up looking like this tomorrow, Hugo will fire me before I even start."

"Maybe we can fix it," Quinn said.

"I was hoping you'd say that. I couldn't go shopping looking like this so I asked Joan Yellowhair, that nice Navajo woman who lives next door, to pick up some dye for me at the market."

Linda Lou stopped crying but the whites of her eyes were so red they clashed with her hair color. She dumped two boxes of hair dye from her tote onto the table—one dark red and one black.

"Let's try the dark red," Quinn said.

"Okay. Honestly, I was afraid to try coloring it myself again after this disaster." She ran her fingers under her hair lifting the sides up and straight out. Her head looked like a giant orange-winged bat.

"Don't worry. We'll fix it."

"I hope so." Her bottom lip quivered.

Quinn took the instructions out of the box and began reading. "Maybe we should start with a strand test. I've never done a dye job before."

"We don't have time to sit around for half an hour. It can't get worse than it is. Just do it."

Quinn slipped on the awkward shaped plastic gloves that came with the hair coloring. She took two bottles of ingredients from the box and mixed them together. Starting at the roots she worked the dye into the glaring orange tresses. After the color was applied, she placed the plastic bag from the kit over Linda Lou's hair, twisted the front tightly, and secured it with a hair clip.

"You're such a good friend to do this for me," Linda Lou said. "I'd die if Hugo saw me like this."

For the next thirty minutes, the women drank coffee and speculated about Bunny's mysterious new boyfriend.

The timer beeped.

Quinn held her breath as she removed the plastic bag. Her eyes narrowed. "Why don't you go rinse it out in the sink," she said. "Then we'll take a look at the finished product."

Linda Lou gave her hair a good rinsing paying special attention to the roots. She returned to the table and looked at Quinn expectantly. "Well?"

Quinn picked up a few strands and closely examined them. "Your hair is definitely not orange but maybe we should try the black dye," her voice sounded upbeat but her face told a different story.

"What's the matter, sweetie?"

"It's purple."

Chapter Fourteen

Quinn glanced at the mirror inside the elevator. She straightened the pearls Megan had given her for Christmas so that they nestled neatly into the neckline of her blouse. Today seemed an especially good day to wear them since she was meeting with lawyer Hugo Smithpepper. Tucked under her right arm was a file containing the information he needed to complete the transfer of Uncle Sean's vacation home into her name.

The law office was located on the third-floor of an old brick office building in downtown Farmington. Quinn did not know what to expect but when the elevator doors opened she was impressed. The office space was upscale with fine cherry furniture and oak floors covered with Persian area rugs. Classical paintings decorated the walls.

Either Smithpepper has a thriving practice or a huge bank debt.

Fresh flowers sat on the corner of the reception desk. She expected to see Linda Lou sitting there but instead an attractive blonde looked up at her. Several secretaries were working nearby but there was no sign of her friend.

Surely, she wasn't fired over the color of her hair.

"May I help you?" the blonde cordially offered.

"I'm Quinn O'Connor."

"Oh, yes. Mr. Smithpepper is expecting you. Follow me, please."

The receptionist led her down a short hallway into a waiting area. Massive wood doors covered most of the far wall of the space. In front of them sat an empty secretary's desk. The woman directed her to a chair near the desk.

"Have a seat. Mr. Smithpepper will be right with you," she said and left.

Before Quinn could sit the huge doors burst open and Linda Lou pranced out looking sophisticated in a gray designer suit. Not even the purple streaks in her now black hair detracted from her professional air.

"Wow, you look great," Quinn said.

"I'm back in my secretary mode." Linda Lou twirled around in her high-heeled shoes. "Thank goodness, I kept some of my working clothes."

"I didn't know you were a legal secretary."

"Oh, I thought I told you. I worked for Jeb Martin for years. When he sold his practice to Hugo, I got a nice severance package. So, I retired."

"You're always so busy—I'm surprised you went back to work."

"Hugo called me a few weeks ago and said he was shorthanded. I didn't have the heart to turn him down. Besides, I figured I could always use a few extra bucks."

A short, portly man with a ruddy face emerged from the office and approached Quinn.

"You must be Mrs. O'Connor. I'm Hugo Smithpepper," he said, taking her hand. "I'm sure we can settle your business without any problems. Did you bring the papers I asked requested?"

"Yes." Quinn handed him the folder.

"Now Hugo, you take good care of my friend if you know what's good for you," Linda Lou said. She leaned over and whispered into Quinn's ear, "He likes my purple streaks."

Despite his complexion, Quinn thought she detected a slight blush on Hugo's face.

"Let's have lunch," Linda Lou offered after Quinn's meeting ended. "There's a nice little spot just down the block from here."

Mary's Downtown Café was bustling with lunch customers when Quinn and Linda Lou arrived. They wandered through the maze of tables and found an empty one in the back corner.

"Well?" Linda Lou fluffed her hair. "What do you think of Hugo?"

"He seems competent enough. He said it would be a simple matter to transfer the title." Quinn surveyed the menu. "What's good?"

"Just about everything except the salads. Mary puts all those exotic greens and sprouts in them like they do at the fancy restaurants. Give me old-fashioned iceberg lettuce any day of the week. I'm not the thistle eating type." She scrunched up her nose. "But I meant, what do you think of Hugo as a man?"

"He's nice." Quinn saw Linda Lou smile and quickly added, "Now, don't you go trying to set me up. He's a lawyer and I was married to a lawyering scoundrel for too long. Besides, he's really not my type."

"Don't worry, you're safe." The smile didn't leave Linda Lou's lips.

"What's the story with you two, anyway?"

"Oh, we go way back. He lived next door to me when we were kids. Our mothers were best friends. Hugo was two years behind me in school. He used to try to look up my skirt in elementary school until I whacked him good a couple of times." She snickered. "In high school, he helped me with algebra and I helped him in square dance class—he was the most uncoordinated thing you ever saw. We've been good friends for years, he's a real sweetheart."

"What would you ladies like?" a freckled-faced waitress asked holding her ordering pad.

Linda Lou cleared her throat and glanced at the menu. "The chicken sandwich looks good, and give me an iced tea."

"I'll have the same." Quinn waited for the waitress to leave. "You know, Hugo blushed when you spoke to him in the office today. Did you two ever have a thing for each other?"

"Heaven's no, he's younger than me. Back in the day it just wasn't done. No self-respecting high school girl would be caught dead with a younger boy." Linda Lou squirmed in her chair and avoided Quinn's eyes.

"I meant more recently."

"Certainly not," she said, continuing to avoid eye contact.

"I don't believe you. Come on, fess up."

"Well," Linda Lou brushed a stray purple strand of hair from her forehead, "I have to admit the thought has crossed my mind once or twice."

"And ... "

"He asked me out once when he was in college, but I was engaged to that deadbeat husband of mine back then. So, I turned him down. It was probably the biggest mistake of my life."

"And now?"

"We're both too old and have a lot of baggage. I'm just helping an old friend out until he can find another secretary," Linda Lou said.

"It looks to me like he has plenty of secretaries in his office."

Their lunch arrived and Linda Lou sipped on her iced tea.

"I'll bet you five dollars Hugo makes a move on you by the end of the month," Quinn said before taking a bite of her sandwich.

"I'll take that sucker bet, sweetie. There's no way he's going to ask me out."

Thursday afternoon Quinn joined Bunny at the fitness center for the second half of their weekly workout.

"It's too bad Linda Lou has to work on Thursdays. I miss her company," Bunny said. She increased the incline on her treadmill and stepped back on.

"Actually, I think she enjoys being around Hugo." Quinn continued to speed walk on the next treadmill. "You know, I think I'm getting better at this," she puffed. "I haven't broken a sweat yet."

"That means it's time to turn up the speed." Bunny smiled. "Linda Lou has always had a thing for Hugo. She just never would admit it to anyone, including herself."

"Well, I think the feeling is mutual. I made a bet with her that he's going to ask her out." Quinn took her towel off the control panel and hung it around her neck.

"I sure hope he does. It would be good for both of them. Say, what are you doing this weekend?"

"I'm not going to Jake's, if that's what you have in mind."

"No, I was thinking that you need to see some of the interesting spots around here." Bunny checked the timer. "Only ten more minutes," she said.

"Which spots?"

"I thought you, Linda Lou, and I might take a trip out to Hart Canyon. It's only a few miles from where you live."

"What's out there?"

"That's where a flying saucer was supposedly found back in 1948."

"Really, I thought the only UFO landing in New Mexico was in Roswell."

"Oh, no. New Mexico was a hotbed of UFO happenings back then and this area was visited several times over the course of a couple years. For three days in 1950, hundreds of people reported seeing flying saucers or some kind of strange flying aircraft zooming over Farmington. My dad swore to his dying day that he saw them all three days."

"Sounds like it might be an interesting place to see. Sure, I'd like to go."

"Good. I'll call Linda Lou to see if she can come along and I'll pack us a picnic lunch."

Bunny drove along the washboard gravel road that snaked through oil and gas well sites in Hart Canyon. She followed the left fork, turned left again up a small hill and entered an empty graded parking area. The only indication they might be in the right place was a large pink arrow with the word *PATH* in big letters.

"Are you sure this is the right spot?" Linda Lou asked Bunny getting out of the car.

"Yep, I'm sure. I've been here before. But I think we should have our lunch first and then hike down to the site."

"Hike? You didn't say anything about a hike." Linda Lou scowled.

"I'll help set up the lawn chairs," Quinn offered attempting to change the mood of the discussion as she walked toward the back of the car.

"Thanks," Bunny said, ignoring Linda Lou. She opened the trunk, took out the ice chest, and handed out the sandwiches and drinks.

Linda Lou stared at Bunny. "Tell me again, why is it we're having a picnic out here in this godforsaken parking lot?" She bent over the side of her lawn chair and picked up her can of soda from the ground.

"Well, the UFO site isn't that far but you probably wouldn't want to carry the chairs and lunch down the path. That's why we're eating here. Besides we need to take in the whole experience— feel the cosmic significance of this whole area." Bunny took a deep breath and spread her arms out with her palms up."

Quinn thought she looked like one of those New Age groupies that meet over in Sedona. "Well, I don't see much to take in," she said. "It looks just like the side of the road over by my place."

"You two are missing the whole point. Something of intergalactic importance happened out here. A flying saucer with little humanoids inside was discovered. It changed our perception of the universe. We are not alone."

"What do you mean by *humanoids*?" Quinn asked before taking a bite of her ham and cheese sandwich.

"This guy, Frank Scully, wrote about it in his book, *Beyond the Flying Saucers*." She rested her chin on the back of her hand for a moment. "You know, I'm sure they named that Scully character in *The X-Files* after him. Anyway, he said there were sixteen little bodies all about three feet tall found dead inside an undamaged spacecraft out here."

"You don't believe all that nonsense, do you Bunny?" Linda Lou wrinkled her forehead and narrowed her eyes.

"Well, I'm not sure I don't believe it. Besides, Jim says there's a lot of people around here who think it's true."

"Jim?" Linda Lou looked at Quinn, "Could this be the mystery man she won't tell us anything about?"

Bunny bristled. "I've said too much already." She folded her arms, pushed her glassed back with her pointer finger, and gazed at the horizon.

"Well, we'd be interested in meeting this Jim. Wouldn't we, Quinn?"

"Yep, we sure would."

"You'll just have to wait until the time is right," Bunny continued to look into the distance.

"Oh, so Jim is the mystery man. Let's see, could it be Jim Johnson, Jim Davis or Jim Templeton?" Linda Lou pressed.

"You know, Linda Lou, the friends of those little aliens could come back looking for them at any moment," Bunny replied. "Maybe we should go down to the site before they return and capture us."

"Oh, she's so good at changing the subject, isn't she?" Linda Lou looked at Quinn.

"She sure is, but I don't think we're going to get any more information about Jim out of her today." Quinn smiled at Bunny who seemed to appreciate getting off the hook. "Say, what happened to the spaceship and all the little bodies?"

"I'll tell you all about it on the way to the site."

The trio walked to the sign and started down the path. At the bottom of a small slope they stopped.

"Which way?" Quinn asked.

Bunny looked around. "There used to be an arrow pointing the way. Wait, there it is."

"Where?" Quinn's eyes searched the area.

"Hanging from that tree." Bunny pointed to a barely visible weathered arrow wired to a branch of an old tree.

"How do you know that's the way? It doesn't say anything." Linda Lou looked disgusted.

"Because I know."

"Well, I hope the rest of the directions are easier to find." Linda Lou lost her footing and slid down the rock strewn decline below the arrow. "Shit!"

"Don't be such a baby," Bunny said. "Well, Scully says all the evidence was carted off to Wright Patterson Air Force Base for study. Other people say everything was taken under cover of night up to a naval facility in Los Alamos."

"And other people, think all those people are crazy," Linda Lou said.

The vague trail led them through small gullies and between trees and scrubs. They passed through a barbed wire gate, onto a mountain bike trail, and along the edge of a small cliff. After about a quarter of a mile, a sign with an alien poking his head out of a flying saucer marked the UFO site.

"We're here!" Bunny chittered and led them to a small commemorative plaque explaining the significance of the site.

"It just looks like a big flat solid rock area," Quinn said.

"But look, you can see old scorching on the rock. It's probably left over from the landing," Bunny said.

"It's probably left over from people building fires out here," Linda Lou said.

"Let's all sit in the middle for a few minutes," Bunny rushed to the center of the area.

The three sat cross-legged forming a circle on the rock.

"Now, close your eyes and contemplate the universe."

"I think I've had enough cosmic experiences for today," Linda Lou said gasping for air as she emerged from the path.

"I didn't realize it was going to be all uphill coming back," Quinn added. She grabbed a bottle of water from the ice chest and gulped it down. "I'm ready to go home."

The women gathered their trash and returned the lawn chairs and ice chest the trunk. They piled into the car with Quinn riding shotgun and Linda Lou stretched out with her feet on the seat in the back.

"Darn this car!" Bunny said as the ignition growled. "It won't start."

"You mean we're stuck out here in alien land?" Linda Lou asked. "Maybe we should look under the hood. Quinn, do you know anything about cars?"

"I don't have the foggiest notion of what to look for. How about you, Bunny?"

"No, I don't even know how to check the oil. What are we going to do? I don't know anyone to call to come help us."

"How about Jim? Why can't your mystery man come to our rescue?" Linda Lou sounded perturbed. She glared at Bunny and sighed.

"He's out of town."

"Oh, sure. Just when we need him," Linda Lou scoffed.

"You two are about the only people I know around here," Quinn said. "Maybe we should call 911."

"Don't be ridiculous. This is not a 911 type of emergency. I'll call Hugo. He's always been a wizard with cars." Linda Lou took her cell phone from her purse and got out of the car. She walked several yards to the edge of the parking lot and made the call.

"I'll bet she's laying on the sweet talk," Bunny said. "I sure hope it works."

Linda Lou walked confidently back to the car. "He's coming."

"How sweet of him." Bunny smiled. "He's always been such a nice guy."

"But you better get the lawn chairs back out. He can't get here until after six o'clock," Linda Lou added.

"Oh, dear!" Bunny frowned.

"What's wrong now?" Linda Lou snapped.

"I have to pee and there is no way I can wait hours," Bunny whined.

Linda Lou pointed down the path. "Find a bush."

Chapter Fifteen

Linda Lou set up her lawn chair a few yards from the car. "We should have brought our bathing suits. We could get a nice tan sitting out here all day." She leaned back in the chair and extended her legs. "Do we have any food left?" she asked Bunny who was standing beside the trunk.

"Half a package of cookies but we have plenty of bottled water. I always keep extra in my trunk. You never know when you're going to get stuck somewhere."

"You mean like now?" Linda Lou rolled her eyes at Quinn.

Bunny placed her hands on her hips. "Just like now, and aren't you two glad I think ahead."

"Maybe some aliens will come and keep us company," Linda Lou said.

"Well, if they do, at least we can offer them water," Quinn said, carrying her chair over to where Linda Lou was sitting."

"… and intergalactic friendship." Bunny spread her arms palms up.

"Get your butt over here and bring the cookies." Linda Lou motioned for Bunny to join them.

"Don't eat them all at once. We're going to be here for a while," Quinn said.

They each took a cookie and decided to save the rest for later.

Bunny snapped up in her chair. "Did you hear that?"

"I didn't hear anything," Linda Lou said.

"Neither did I," Quinn added.

"Well, listen. There's something rummaging around in that bush over there." She pointed to a rather large scrub on the edge of the parking area.

"Jeez, what is it?" Quinn squealed as a scruffy fur nose poked round the edge of the bush.

Bunny jumped to her feet. "I don't know, but it sure doesn't look like a kitty cat."

"Stop!" Linda Lou tried to block Bunny with her arm. "Don't go any closer."

"What do you think I am, a fool? I'm heading for the car." Before Bunny could move, a menacing gray animal emerged from behind the bush. "Yikes!" she said, dancing in place.

"Pipe down and don't move," Linda Lou whispered firmly. "It looks like a large coyote."

"Maybe if we yell, we'll scare it away," Quinn offered.

"And maybe not." Linda Lou stiffened her neck. "It could be rabid."

The animal began to circle toward them.

"We need a plan, any plan," Bunny said.

"Someone needs to lure him away. We can use the cookies as bait." Quinn grabbed the package from Bunny.

"I'll do it," Linda Lou said, "If he charges, I can run faster than you two." She thought for a moment. "I'll get his attention by spreading a trail of broken cookies out of the parking lot and up the road a bit. You guys head back to the car, but go real slow and don't turn your backs on him."

"Then what?" Bunny shifted nervously side to side.

"I'll start back when I have one cookie left. I'll get as close to him as is safe and throw it in his direction. Hopefully, that will whet his appetite for something other than us. Then, I'll head for the car. Have the door open so I can hop in if he comes after me."

"Maybe the cookies will distract him enough that he'll just wander off," Quinn said.

"Let's hope so." Linda Lou took the cookies from Quinn and walked a few feet toward the animal. She tossed bits of cookie behind her as she casually strolled toward the road—all the time keeping one eye on the gaunt beast.

The creature kept a keen watch but did not follow her. Linda Lou circled back and threw the last cookie right under his nose. He gobbled up the offering and set off after the rest of the bait.

"Thank goodness it worked," Bunny sighed as Linda Lou hopped into the car and slammed the door.

"I wouldn't be so quick to judge. Here he comes back." Quinn pointed out the car window.

The predator bounded toward the car and posted itself about three feet away.

"He thinks we have more food," Linda Lou said.

"Try honking the horn," Quinn suggested. "Maybe that will scare him."

Bunny blasted the horn three times. The animal bared his teeth and cocked his head to one side.

Linda Lou cracked open the window and yelled "Shoo, shoo, go away!"

The beast took two quick steps toward the car before she could get the window back up.

The women sat silently in the hot car for the next half hour.

"I'm parched. Is there any water in here?" Quinn asked.

"Only in the trunk, and I don't think it's a good idea to get out and retrieve it," Linda Lou said.

"Oh, dear," Bunny said. "You mentioned water and now I have to pee."

"Well, hold it," Linda Lou snapped.

The crafty carnivore held them at bay the rest of the afternoon.

A few minutes after six, Hugo's car zoomed up the road. The animal turned and hightailed it out of sight as the car rolled to a stop.

Bunny swung open the front passenger door. She dashed for the path and the bush she had visited earlier.

"Where's she going?" Hugo asked as he walked up to their car.

"Taking care of business," Quinn answered.

Hugo laughed. "I see you girls decided to wait in the car." He leaned on the open door. "I hope you didn't feed that mangy oil field dog I saw running up the road."

"Dog?" the two women said in unison.

He walked to the front of the car, lifted the hood and surveyed the situation. "Looks like a loose battery cable to me."

"Is that bad?" Bunny asked returning from the bush.

"It'll just take a minute to fix." He took a wrench from his trunk and tightened the cable. "That ought to do it. Give it a try."

Bunny turned the ignition key and the car started. "Thanks Hugo, you're a real lifesaver."

Three days later, Bunny enrolled in a two-week basic auto maintenance course at the college.

"I'm never going to feel that stupid again," she told Quinn. "Why don't you sign up? We can learn together."

"It's not my thing."

"You'll be sorry one of these days."

"You know, Bunny, I really admire the way you go after what you want without worrying about what other people think."

"What do you mean?"

"Like they way you had the guts to find a man and how you don't mind if Linda Lou gets on your case about believing in UFO's.

"Well, if you don't live your life the way you want, there's no one to blame but yourself."

If only I could live my life that way. But my life's not so bad. I can sit out on my deck whenever I want and read or listen to the sounds of nature. I can close my eyes and breathe the clean fresh air. And the tension and anger I've felt for so long is appearing less often.

After Thursday's workout, Quinn stopped by the post office and found another postcard from Megan. The cards had been arriving every few days for the last two weeks. The first card had a picture of Macy's department store on the front. Scrawled across the face of the building in felt tip marker was "Got your dress yet?" Philadelphia's famous Love sculpture was on Monday's card with "Love is in the air. See you soon" written on the back. Today's card had a photo of the Liberty Bell and said, "Don't forget to liberate me from planning this wedding alone."

Megan always found unique ways to get her points across—like the time she drove Patrick's riding lawnmower to high school after he told her she didn't need a car. That weekend he bought her a beat up silver Toyota which lasted her all the way through college.

I'd better make my reservations soon or it's anyone's guess what she might do.

After leaving the post office, she stopped at Abe's and bought four little packages of butter crunch toffee with chocolate and almonds. She polished them off on her way home.

The telephone was ringing when she walked into the courtyard. She hurried inside the house and picked up the kitchen phone.

"Hey, birthday girl, what are you up to?" Eddy's sunny voice asked.

"It's not my birthday yet. I still have a few days before the big 5–0."

"What are you doing right now?"

"I'm not doing anything. I just walked in the door." Quinn opened the fridge. Feeling guilty about the toffee, she took out a can of diet root beer and popped the top.

"Why don't you walk back out the door and come pick me up at the airport?"

"What?"

"I'm at the Farmington airport."

"You're here?"

"That's right. I couldn't let my best friend celebrate her fiftieth birthday alone, could I?"

"I'm on my way—can't wait to see you."

"Give me a minute and I'll have the margaritas ready," Quinn said when they returned from the airport. "Go stash your suitcase in the extra bedroom and I'll meet you out on the deck."

Eddy stretched out on the chaise lounge and enjoyed the view. "I love the way the sunlight shimmers off the cottonwoods leaves," she said when Quinn handed her a margarita.

"It is pretty out here this time of year. How long can you stay?"

"I'm leaving tomorrow."

"Oh, no. You can't leave so soon," Quinn said. "You just got here."

Eddy grinned. "I'm leaving, and so are you."

"Wait, I can't ..."

"Yes, you can. You're coming with me. I'm taking you away for a birthday surprise."

"New York? Are we going to New York to see a Broadway show?" Quinn's eyes widened as she sat in a patio chair next to Eddy.

"We're going to New York, but we are not stopping there." Eddy looked smug. "And, we are going to see a show, but not on Broadway."

"Oh, stop with the riddles and tell me what's up."

"Sam Maxwell is filming a movie in Paris, but you probably already know that."

"And?" Quinn took a sip of her drink.

"I thought we'd drop in and pay him a little visit."

"In Paris, France?"

"Well duh, not Paris, Texas. We're going to celebrate your birthday in style. We're staying at the Ritz, shopping for designer clothes, and taking in a show at the Lido. While we're sightseeing, we'll try to find out where Sam is filming. How's that for a birthday present?"

"Wow!"

"Now, get me another margarita and go start packing. We're leaving at ten tomorrow morning."

Chapter Sixteen

Quinn was exhausted from the full day of travel it took to get to New York. But her adrenaline kicked in as she and Eddy settled into their seats in the first class section of the flight to Paris.

"We need to get some sleep," Eddy said, "or jet lag will get us when we arrive."

"I know, but I'm wide awake." Quinn looked around the cabin.

A man seated a few rows up caught her attention. He looked out of place with his torn jeans, dirty sneakers, and unkempt hair. She turned to point him out to Eddy but her friend was already asleep. Quinn took a Tony Hillerman novel out of her purse and began reading.

"When are we going to get some food around here," a man's harsh voice boomed.

Quinn looked up and saw it was the grungy man lambasting the flight attendant.

An hour later she heard him start up again.

"... and I want another Scotch," he shouted.

"I'm sorry sir, but I can't serve you any more drinks," the flight attendant said in a calm voice.

The man cursed.

"Sir, if you don't settle down, I'll have to call the captain."

What a jerk! Quinn returned her attention to the novel. Too tired to keep her eyes open she fell asleep.

It felt like Quinn had entered a Tower of Babel when she disembarked from the flight and entered Orly Airport. The international chatter made her long to hear only English.

"It's always like this," Eddy said. "Sometimes you can hardly hear yourself think."

The women made their way through the throng of passengers to the customs area and stood in line waiting their turn to pass through. A few feet ahead officials began searching the bags of a straggly-haired man who looked to be in his mid-forties.

"Do you know who I am?" the man demanded in a loud voice.

Quinn immediately recognized him as the overblown jerk from the plane.

"Let me through. I have an important business meeting to get to and you are holding me up," the man protested with a scowl.

"*Monsieur*, you will be here even longer if you do not cooperate," the official in charge replied.

"It's people like that Neanderthal that give Americans a bad name in France," Eddy muttered.

In a few minutes, the women passed through the line and headed for the exit. Quinn slung the strap of her carry-on bag over the handle of her gray suitcase and pulled it toward the curb. The limousine Eddy ordered was waiting for them. The uniformed driver rushed to open the door and the two scurried inside.

"*Ritz Paris, s'il vous plait*," Eddy told him when he finished loading their suitcases.

Forty-five minutes later, their limousine glided to a stop in front of the luxury hotel. The hundred year old structure was located on the beautiful Place Vendôme. It was a magnificent piece of architecture and Quinn could not help gaping at the façade.

A doorman with fringed epaulets on his blue coat snapped his fingers and ordered a muscular bellman to retrieve their belongings. He ushered the women through the polished brass revolving door of the main entrance and into the lobby.

"I'll check us in. Be back in a minute." Eddy gave Quinn a little wave and walked toward the front desk.

Quinn flopped into a plush velvet armchair located between a large potted palm and an ornate end table. She considered taking off her shoes but the sight of the proper, exquisitely dressed guests in the lobby made her think twice about the idea. She took the Hillerman novel out of her purse and began reading.

Eddy marched back, a frown on her face. "I'm so disappointed."

Quinn placed her bookmark between the pages and set the novel on the table. "What's wrong?"

"The Elton John Suite is unavailable, so they put us in a regular one. They warned me when I made the reservation that someone was occupying it and might still be here when we arrived."

"I'm sure a regular suite will be fine."

"Damn, I really wanted to stay in the Elton John."

"Do you think he actually stays there?" Quinn asked and got up from the chair.

"Sure," Eddy replied. "They say he even helped decorate the place."

"I wonder if someone as famous as him is staying there now."

"I doubt it. Probably some über-rich oil guy from the Middle East. They love this hotel." Eddy handed the room number to the bellman and the women trailed after him.

Inside their suite Eddy gave the man a generous tip and thanked him for placing the bags in their bedrooms.

"I'm going to unpack and change clothes," Eddy said.

Quinn looked around the suite. Rich silk and brocade fabrics decorated the elegant sitting room. A fruit basket and a bottle of

French wine rested on the table next to over-sized windows that looked down on the lush hotel gardens.

"Hey, there's a bottle of wine out here," she called. "Let's have a drink after we unpack."

A huge tapestry of Renaissance angels hung over the head of the bed in Quinn's room. In the bathroom, Carrara marble covered most of the surfaces and there was a Jacuzzi tub and a bidet.

Wow, I can't believe this place, she said to herself. *If this is a regular suite, I wonder what the Elton John Suite looks like.* She stepped back into the bedroom. The bed looked like a person could get lost in it. A lovely upholstered bench sat at its foot. She lifted her suitcase onto the bench and started unpacking.

"Crap!" she flung her hands into the air and stomped her right foot.

Eddy rushed into the room. "What's wrong?"

"How could I be so stupid?" Her eyebrows lowered. She hurled her carry-on bag onto the bed and began rummaging through it.

"What is it?"

"I forgot to pack my panties. I can't find a single pair anywhere." Quinn sat slump shouldered on the edge of the bed.

Raising a hand to her mouth, Eddy let out a horrified gasp. But, as she lowered her hand, Quinn could see her friend had been hiding a smile.

"By the sound of your voice, I thought it was something serious," Eddy chortled.

"You don't call this serious? I have no panties."

"This is Paris, city of romance. I'm sure we can buy some great panties here."

"Oh yeah, and what am I supposed to do in the meantime? It's too late to go shopping," she groaned. "I guess I'll have to wash out the ones I have on and hope they dry by morning."

"You're in France." Eddy began chanting the childhood refrain, *"Oh, the girls in France, they don't wear underpants."*

"Maybe French girls don't, but I do."

Eddy left the room and returned a minute later. She tossed a wadded ball in Quinn's direction.

"What's this?" she asked catching it with one hand.

"Panties. Brand-new ones, bought especially for this trip. Now they're yours, so quit whining."

Quinn straightened out the bundle. "They're black lace and ... oh, it's a thong. I've never worn anything like this."

"Girl, it's about time you started. And tomorrow we'll go shopping for more of the same."

"Okay, okay. Let's have that drink," Quinn said. She walked back into the sitting room.

"I'll open the bottle," Eddy said. "This fruit looks good, want a piece?"

Quinn's purse was on the table next to the basket of fruit. "Oh gosh," she said and rushed to look inside.

"What are you looking for?"

"I think I might have left my book in the lobby." She rummaged around in the purse. "It's not here."

"You can get another copy, can't you?"

"It's not the book I'm worried about. My grandfather's bookmark was inside. I'm going downstairs to see if I can find it." She hurried out of the room.

Eddy opened the wine and poured a glass.

Twenty minutes later, Quinn returned looking gloomy. "It wasn't there." She collapsed onto the sofa with her face in her hands. "I shouldn't have been so careless. It was the only thing of his I had."

"Did you check at the desk?"

"Yes, but it hadn't been turned in."

After breakfast, Quinn and Eddy set out for Alice Cadolle's lingerie shop. With Eddy's coaxing, Quinn purchased enough outrageously provocative panties to last the entire trip. She even added a few coordinating bras.

"When you're in France, you need to be prepared for a *tête-à-tête* with a stranger," Eddy instructed in the dressing room while trying on a black silk and lace demi-bra.

"You won't catch me messing around with a stranger," Quinn said.

"Oh? Believe me there's nothing like a sweaty, sizzling night in the Elton John Suite with someone you'll never see again." She bent over and wiggled her shoulders exposing her pink areolas over the edge of the lace cups. "How do I look?"

"Provocative. So, you had a hidden agenda in wanting that suite?"

"I just wanted to recall a sexy encounter."

"Tell me about him. Come on, give it up."

"There are some things a girl keeps to herself," she moaned and licked her lips before laughing.

Eddy set four shopping bags filled with purchases on the table in the sitting room of the suite. "I'm hungry, want to go downstairs and get some lunch?"

"No. I'm exhausted. I think I'll stay here and soak in the tub, nibble on some fruit, and take a little nap before dinner." Quinn sank into the brocade sofa.

"Okay. After lunch, I'm going to peruse the shops down the street. How about I meet you for dinner at that cute little restaurant, Café Germaine, we saw this morning? Say, about six?" Eddy picked up her Chanel handbag and headed for the door.

"Sounds good to me."

Eddy stood outside the elevator door waiting for a ride to the lobby. She twisted the three-stone diamond ring on her right hand and fidgeted. Elevators always made her nervous. Once in Italy she was stuck alone inside one for two hours. Since then claustrophobia hit her every time she stepped inside one. Still, she wasn't about to walk by herself down several flights of stairs.

The elevator opened, she took a deep breath and stepped across the threshold joining two other people in the compartment. She watched the floor indicator all the way down. When the doors opened at the lobby, she sprinted out and sighed in relief.

Uneasiness crept over her as she walked along the corridor leading to the restaurant.

"I see you weren't able to hijack the elevator like you hijacked my cab," a man's voice taunted.

She did not think the man was talking to her, but quickened her pace anyway.

A strong hand clasped her arm and pulled her into a shadowy alcove. "You didn't think you could get away from me, did you?" The man spun her around to face him.

"It's you!" Eddy was eyeball-to-eyeball with Cigar Man. "Let me go!" She tried to pull her arm free but his hold was solid. "What do you want?"

"I want to talk to you," he said in a low intimidating voice.

"I don't have anything to talk to you about." She tried again to pull her arm free.

"Just hang on a minute." He tightened his grip.

"Why are you doing this? You're hurting me," she blurted.

"It's business." His eyes narrowed.

"What sort of business?"

"My business." He pulled her closer. "Why are you following me? You were at my hotel in the Bahamas, and now in Paris. Hell, I even thought I saw you in a bar in L.A. Who's paying you to spy on me? What do they want, information on my next project?"

"You've got to be kidding."

"Lady, I don't kid."

"Well, maybe you need to lighten up." She wondered if she had misspoken and forced a smile to regain her confidence. "You're not the only person who travels around the world, you know. Where's your nasty cigar?"

"I'm trying to quit," the tone of his voice softened.

She looked him over—dark piercing eyes, firm jaw, and strong hands with manicured fingernails.

"Why are you looking at me like that?" he asked seemingly taken aback.

She put her arms around his neck and kissed him before he had a chance to react. "What are you doing the rest of the afternoon?" she cooed.

He pressed his lips hard against her neck and whispered in her ear with a husky voice, "Everything."

Cigar Man lay on his back with his head propped on a pillow and his eyes riveted on Eddy as she dressed.

"Need a cigar?" she teased.

"I don't have the urge for one, but I have a powerful urge for you." He rolled onto his side. "Damn you woman, you're my age. I usually go for young women with firm tits and tight asses."

"And I like men with rock-hard abs," she sassed back.

"Guess I deserved that. How can a woman as irritating as you can feel so good?"

Eddy bent over and slid the heel strap of her pump into place. She saw his body stir again."

"Don't go yet," he said.

"I have to, I'm really late. See you around, ah …" She searched his face, pretending she did not know his name.

"Marty … Marty Winter is my name."

"I'm Eddy." She picked up her Chanel handbag and walked out of the Elton John Suite.

Chapter Seventeen

Quinn gazed through the windows of Café Germaine. Across the Seine, she could discern some of the intricate details of the spire and towers of Notre Dame de Paris. The cathedral's bell tolled six times.

Where's Eddy? she wondered.

The front door of the café creaked open. Quinn turned to see an elderly man and woman enter. She glanced at her watch for the fourth time in five minutes.

"Would you like a glass of wine, *Madame?*" a short, rotund waiter asked.

"*Oui.* A glass of cabernet sauvignon, *s'il vous plait.*" She marveled at how he managed to glide his considerable girth between the closely placed tables.

In a few minutes he returned with the wine. "Are you ready to order?"

"Not yet. I'm expecting a friend."

"Very well, *Madame.*" Leaving two menus he sailed away.

Quinn savored the robust wine, watched couples as they passed by the café, and let her mind drift.

Looking up the street she spied a long-limbed man walking by himself. A herringbone hat was pulled low over his forehead. As he drew closer, she noticed there was something in his hand.

She set her glass on the table and strained to get a better look, but could not make out what he was carrying.

The man made a quick turn at the door and entered the café. He was holding a book with a golden tassel dangling from its pages. With downcast eyes, he maneuvered his way through the narrow aisle heading for an empty table. As he squeezed past Quinn, his knee jostled her table.

She grabbed too late for her wineglass. The scarlet liquid spewed across the white linen tablecloth. She lurched from her chair. The wine narrowly missed her dress and dripped onto the floor splattering her shoes.

"*Excusez-moi, Madame.*"

Quinn looked up from her shoes and into the face of Sam Maxwell. Her knees grew weak and several seconds passed before she was able to speak.

"It's okay. I didn't get any on my dress, just on my feet." She tried to smile but her face felt frozen in place.

"I'm so glad you speak English. I really don't know how to properly apologize in French." He looked flustered. "I ... I'll get someone to take care of this." He waved the waiter over to the table.

"Ah, *Madame*. Your friend has arrived?" The waiter winked and smiled, but Quinn ignored him.

"Please, can you bring a towel and change the tablecloth?" Sam asked before ordering the most expensive bottle of wine on the menu.

"Really, it isn't necessary to order wine," she said relaxing a little.

"It's the least I can do after the mess I caused."

"Then would you like to join me for a glass?" Quinn shuddered—she had just invited Sam Maxwell to have a drink with her.

"Good idea." He smiled. "Sam Maxwell."

"Quinn O'Connor." She extended her hand. "It's nice to meet you." Her insides melted at his touch. "Please, sit down," she said.

"Have we met before?" he asked. "You look familiar." He placed his book on the table and sat across from her. "Honestly, I'm not handing you a line. I just have a strange feeling that I know you. I'm an actor. Have we worked together?"

"No. Not really."

"Not really?"

"Well, I was an extra in *Turquoise Trail* in New Mexico. That's where I live."

"New Mexico," he mused. "I always enjoy going there. Are you an actress?"

"Heavens, no. I'm a high school teacher. Or at least, I used to be. I'm taking some time off."

"My mom was a high school teacher. She loved those kids." He paused as if a pleasant memory returned. "Personally, I don't know how she put up with them for all those years. I remember how rotten I was at sixteen." He flashed a wicked grin.

The waiter returned and spread the clean tablecloth. He placed the bottle of wine and two glasses on the table. Removing a white towel from his shoulder, he said, "Please, *Madame*, let me dry your feet." He got down on one knee. Before she could say a word he had patted her feet dry and left.

"Wow. I bet that felt a bit kinky," Sam said. They both burst out laughing.

Quinn was thankful the conversation had turned away from her stint as a movie extra. *What would he think if he knew I was the woman in the water trough?* She squirmed in her chair and her new bikini panties rode up into an uncomfortable position. She wiggled a bit more to get them back where they belonged. Sam did not seem to notice.

His manner put her at ease. Their conversation flowed effortlessly from subject to subject. Soon the bottle of wine was empty.

"Would you like to join me for a stroll along the Seine, Quinn?" he asked and stood. He reached for his book and knocked it off the table. *The Grapes of Wrath* landed on the floor next to its golden tasseled bookmark. He bent over and retrieved them.

The hand-tooling on the marker was unmistakable. Quinn's heart jumped and her face turned pale.

"What's the matter?"

"I ... I had a bookmark just like that one. I lost it yesterday."

"That's when I found this one, in the lobby of my hotel. It was on the floor next to the chair where I was sitting. I asked around but no one claimed it, so I didn't see any harm in keeping it. Look, it has my initial."

"I'm sure that's my bookmark. My great-grandmother made it for my grandfather," Quinn said. "The *M* is for Maguire."

"A delightful woman like you shouldn't be without her grandfather's bookmark," Sam said handing it to Quinn. He leaned over the tiny table and kissed her on the cheek. "We were destined to meet."

Her face flushed, and this time she knew it wasn't from a hot flash.

"Quinn, Quinn!"

Eddy's voice pulled her from the depths of her Sam Maxwell fantasy.

"What's the matter with you?" Eddy demanded. "Didn't you see me waving at you from the door?"

"I'm sorry. I was thinking about something." Quinn fidgeted with her napkin.

"You mean someone, don't you?" Eddy sat down. "How long have you been waiting?"

"Since around six."

"I'm sorry. Something came up and I couldn't get away. Let's eat."

"You know, this Sam Maxwell thing has really gotten out of hand," Quinn said when the waiter left with their order. "I mean, here I was completely lost in my fantasy when you spoke to me. It was so real. I swear it was like he was sitting right across from me talking. I could even feel the warmth of his touch. I must be going crazy."

"Hey, we all have fantasies."

"Yeah, well why do you think I waited so long to tell Bunny and Linda Lou about Sam? Because they would have thought I was a nut job, that's why."

"I don't think they would have ..."

"Oh, yes they would. I've followed Sam Maxwell halfway around the world. Doesn't that sound crazy to you?"

"I wouldn't call it crazy. I'd call it stealthy—an invisible pursuit. It's like when we followed Mike Sheridan."

"We were fourteen, and we followed him around the bleachers at the football games."

"Well, it's the same principle just on a grander scale. But remember, we didn't come to Paris just to track down Sam Maxwell. We're here to celebrate your birthday—you're fiftieth birthday. It's a milestone. You can do whatever you want on your fiftieth birthday and no one can call you crazy."

"But this whole thing is too weird. I wake up thinking about him. I go to bed and he's the last thing on my mind. He pops into my head at the strangest times like when I'm in line at the grocery store or filling my car with gas. Hard as I try, I can't get him out of my head."

"That could be it. Maybe you're trying too hard to stop thinking about him. If you really want to get him out of your mind—don't try so hard."

"That's ridiculous."

"No, it isn't. When my second husband left me, he was the only thing I could think about. My eyes were so red from crying I went through six bottles of eye drops in two weeks."

"And?"

"And then, I couldn't get over the fact that I couldn't get over him. But when I finally stopped obsessing over not getting over him, that's when I got over him."

"I see, I think." Quinn tapped her fingernails on the table and thought for a few seconds. The painful tingling sensation in her nose told her she would cry if she didn't stop herself.

"You don't think …" Quinn sniffled, "You don't think all this could be connected to Patrick, do you?"

"Patrick?" Eddy looked puzzled.

"I was so mad when I found out he was cheating, I could have killed him. But he was already dead. There wasn't anything I could do to get even. When I moved to New Mexico, I thought I was past my hateful need for revenge."

"So, what's that got to do with Sam Maxwell?"

"It was in New Mexico where the whole Sam thing started. When I watched that blasted movie, passion stirred in me again. I wanted someone to desire me … a great, sexy guy to want only me."

"Please." Eddy swooshed her manicured hand. "There are plenty of great guys who'd go for you in a minute. You're witty, beautiful, and your body still looks good. What's not to want?"

"You're my best friend, you have to say that. I can't explain how awful I felt about myself after Patrick's death. I was sure no man would ever want me. After all, I couldn't even keep my own husband from straying and everyone knew it."

"The cheating was about Patrick. It wasn't about you. He would have cheated on anyone."

"I'm not so sure about that. I should have been woman enough to keep him faithful. Do you think it's possible that to compensate for the loss of Patrick's love I substituted an obsession for Sam—as a sort of survival technique?"

130

"Well, that does make a strange sort of sense."

"So, now what do I do?"

"Beats me."

Around four the next morning, Quinn popped two aspirin and washed them down with a swig of bottled water. Sleep had been elusive. She placed the bottle on the marble vanity top and looked at herself in the bathroom mirror. Her hair was a mess and her eyes were red from crying.

Squinting in the light of the bedside sconce, she shuffled back into the bedroom. At the foot of the bed she paused, her eyes drawn to the tapestry of angels above the headboard.

I can't believe it. A tiny image of the prince of darkness jumped out at her from the lower left corner of the fabric. *It's about the classic struggle—good versus evil—devil or angel. And Lucifer looks a lot like Patrick.*

"There is no way in hell you're going to win, Patrick," she said. "I don't need you to make me feel complete. And I don't need any stupid fantasy about Sam Maxwell either."

131

Chapter Eighteen

Dressed in her nightgown, Quinn shuffled into the sitting room at half past eight the next morning.

"How does it feel to be half a century old, birthday girl?" Eddy teased from the sofa.

"Better than dead," Quinn moaned.

"You look like a wreck."

"I hardly slept a wink. My thoughts kept racing. I couldn't stop thinking about Patrick and Sam. But I've made up my mind. We're not going to waste a minute searching for Sam while we're here." Quinn pursed her lips and flopped onto the sofa next to Eddy.

"And I was so looking forward to an adventure."

"I'm sure you were, but I've decided to act like a grown-up and take responsibility for my own life. And don't you dare breathe a word about Sam Maxwell to Megan or I'll never hear the end of it."

"My lips are sealed." Eddy turned an imaginary key next to her mouth.

Quinn lifted herself out of the sofa and walked over to the massive fireplace. Perched on tiptoes she looked into the gold-framed mirror hanging above it. She pulled down her lower eyelids and groaned.

"Crap, I look like I have pink eye and what am I going to do about my hair?

Eddy stretched her legs out onto the coffee table. "I told you, you looked like a wreck."

"Yeah, but I didn't believe you."

Downstairs at a corner table in L'Espadon Restaurant, Eddy gobbled her scrambled eggs with truffles. "You're not eating. What's wrong?" she asked Quinn.

"I'm just enjoying the atmosphere. This place is so opulent." She poked her fork at the rolled omelet and lobster medallions on her plate and took a bite. "Mmm, this is heavenly."

"We're going sightseeing after breakfast," Eddy announced. "You can't come to Paris and miss the Eiffel Tower or the Louvre. I've hired a limo for the whole day so we can go wherever you want on your birthday."

"You're the best." Quinn smiled at Eddy, took another bite of lobster, and returned to admiring her surroundings. Two figures at a table near the center of the room caught her eye. "Say, isn't that Cigar Man sitting over there?"

Eddy zeroed in on the man. "Yep, that's Marty."

"Marty? Since when did he become Marty?"

"Since ... you don't want to know. Besides, isn't the guy sitting with him the idiot the customs officials detained?"

"Sure looks like him though he certainly has cleaned up."

"I wonder what those two are up to." Eddy raised an eyebrow.

Marty looked up from his breakfast. He smiled and nodded at Eddy.

"Wouldn't you know it—he caught us staring at them." She smiled and gave a little wave before turning to Quinn. "Just act natural and keep talking."

"Okay. Let's go to the Eiffel Tower first. They say you can see all of Paris from up there."

"It's a deal." Eddy glanced at the men out of the corner of her eye. "Maybe they'll be gone by the time we finish eating. I don't want to talk to Marty."

"Why not?"

"Well, we sort of had a thing yesterday."

"So, that's why you were late." Quinn sipped her orange juice. "You're not going to break his heart are you?"

"Hell, no. The man is made of stone. But he's pretty damn good in bed."

"Eddy!" Quinn choked almost spitting her juice onto the table.

"W-what?" Eddy's fake smile beamed.

The men ended their discussion and left the restaurant without finishing their meals.

"At last." Eddy seemed to relax as the men walked out. "Now, I can have my coffee in peace."

Quinn leaned against the railing at the top of the Eiffel Tower. "Look, there's Sacre Coeur," she said, pointing to Monmartre. "It really stands out doesn't it?"

"It's amazing how white it looks even from this distance. Do you see the Louvre across the Seine to the left?" Eddy asked pointing toward the museum.

"I can see a bit of the pyramid."

"We should wait until tomorrow for the Louvre. It takes at least a full day to explore and today's half gone."

"That's fine with me. Let's go shopping. I want to buy myself a few birthday presents." Quinn turned to Eddy. "Are you going to be okay going back down on the elevator? I thought you were going to pass out coming up."

"Well, I'm not going to walk down all those stairs. For this view, I can brave the elevator once in a while. I'll be all right."

Quinn purchased a long silk scarf at Hermes, a pair of red high heels at Yves St. Laurent, and a purple leather handbag at Versace.

"I've never spent this much money on myself before," she said eyeing the receipt for her handbag.

"You only live once and it's time you get with it, girl. Besides, it's not like you can't afford to splurge once in a while," Eddy said. "We've got one more stop to make. I'm buying you a special birthday dress for tonight."

"I don't need a new dress."

"Yes, you do. I don't want to hear another word about it. The matter is settled."

Paris glittered like a pink diamond as they rode in the limousine up the Champs-Elysees toward the Lido. The chauffeur eased to a stop in front of the small entrance to the famous cabaret.

As the driver helped her from the car, Quinn felt the cool night air brush her cheeks. Up the avenue she caught a partial view of the Arc de Triomphe. She bobbed her head trying to see through the large group of the people milling in front of the nightclub but could not get a clear view of the monument.

"Jeez, I've got to get a better look at it," she muttered. Without thinking she scampered into the middle of the street, her tight sheath and three-inch heels forcing her to take chipmunk size steps. Her silver evening bag sparkled as it fluttered from the delicate chain draped over her arm.

"Stop!" Eddy yelled.

Brakes screeched. A black Peugot swerved to miss her. A pinch-faced taxi driver gestured wildly and hurled French profanities through his open window. Traffic came to a stop amid the smell of burning rubber and honking horns.

Quinn stood on the center island staring at the lighted colossus—imprinting the image of in her mind.

"Are you crazy? Get out of there!" Eddy barked.

A moment later, Quinn came to her senses. Startled by the commotion, she walked gingerly back across the street this time checking for traffic.

"I never realized the Arc was so huge. I wish I'd had my camera, I could have gotten a great photo out there."

"We're going inside before you do any more damage." Eddy took her by the arm and pulled her toward the entrance of the club.

Quinn and Eddy settled at their table near the stage.

"These are wonderful seats," Quinn observed.

"Wait until the show starts. This whole section descends, like a giant elevator, to give everyone a better view of the stage."

"Are you okay with that? I know how you are with elevators."

"Oh, sure. I'm fine as long as I'm not closed in." Eddy poured Quinn a glass of champagne. "The show won't start for a while, and nature is calling," she said, getting up from the table.

"Don't worry. I've got the champagne to keep me company." Quinn held up her glass in a mock toast.

In a hurry to get to the powder room, Eddy did not notice Marty Winter in the bar at the rear of the showroom. But on her way back he was directly in her line of sight.

Maybe I should ignore him. Oh, what the hell.

Marty took a hefty swig of his highball as she approached.

"Oh, so now who's following who?" her voice trilled with sarcasm. She sat in the empty chair next to him and rubbed her leg against his.

"Don't give yourself so much credit. I'm here on business," he said and took a large puff from his cigar.

"I thought you were giving up cigars."

He ignored her, took another puff, and blew the smoke into the air.

"At least you didn't blow it in my face this time," she said.

He laughed and took another puff.

"You said you were on business. What kind of business are you on?" She tried to read his eyes.

"My business, but don't let that scare you away," he crooned.

"I don't scare easily."

"No, you don't." He winked at her. "Eddy, this is a business associate of mine, Alastair Applegate." He nodded at the man sitting opposite him.

"Nice to meet you, Alastair," she said, forcing a smile. *He's the same man who was eating breakfast with Marty—the jerk from airport. Alastair Applegate, the name doesn't fit him—probably a pseudonym.*

Alastair acknowledged her with a patronizing bob of his head.

"Can I buy you a drink?" Marty asked.

"Thanks, but I'm with a friend. I have to get back to our table." She shifted her gaze from Marty to his companion, "What business are you in, Alastair?"

"The Arts," he clipped.

Marty chuckled at his companion's vague answer. He placed his hand on Eddy's knee, "Stay a while."

"Can't." She rose from her chair and blew Marty a kiss. "See you later."

Aware of his eyes following her, she strolled down the aisle to rejoin Quinn.

"Sorry I took so long." Sitting, she poured herself a flute of champagne.

"Not to worry. Suddenly, I feel a new sense of freedom and independence coming on. I bet the showgirls really feel free parading around topless."

"Well, don't get any ideas. You've already narrowly escaped arrest once tonight."

The Louvre, Versailles, Notre Dame de Paris, and other sights made a blur of the next three days. After a full day at the Louvre, Eddy seemed afraid they might miss something important. So, she picked up the pace hustling Quinn from site to site.

Looking out the window of their suite, Eddy pouted, "We're leaving tomorrow morning and we haven't had a drink at the Hemingway Bar."

"Jeez, my feet are killing me. Can't we skip that experience?" Quinn pulled off her shoes and massaged her toes. "I need a nap."

"How about we compromise? We'll only stay for an hour."

"Okay, you win. Guess we should dress up a bit, huh?"

After changing they headed for the bar.

"Don't you feel out of place in here? It's so masculine," Quinn said. She examined the rich paneling and photos on the wall.

Eddy leaned back in her leather armchair. "I love this place. I feel like Ernest Hemingway could walk through the door any minute."

"It certainly is impressive." Quinn fixed her eyes on the bartender. A touch of white in his short hair completed his neatly polished appearance. "I'm glad we didn't try to find Sam on this trip. I've had so much fun just going with the flow of things." She took a drink of her Picasso Martini and licked her lips.

"It's been interesting, hasn't it? But, you know, we haven't run into Marty in the last three days."

"You sound disappointed. Maybe he left Paris."

"Not disappointed, just a bit curious. I wonder what he really does for a living." Eddy put her elbow on the table and rested her chin in her hand. "He sure is good at avoiding the subject."

"Maybe he's involved in some illegal international scheme."

"You've been reading too many mystery novels."

"That reminds me. Don't let me forget to check at the front desk to see if anyone turned in my bookmark."

Chapter Nineteen

Quinn opened the gate to the courtyard of her house on the San Juan River and smiled at the familiar clang of the cowbell. The plants lining the wall had turned green while she was away and their buds were beginning to burst open. The cozy space was swept clean and the chairs washed off—no doubt Linda Lou's handiwork.

She plopped down in one of the wooden chairs and watched a sparrow peck at the water in the little birdbath. "Funny," she whispered, "why didn't I take time to watch the birds in California?"

Even though she was dead tired from her trip, the first thing she did after entering the house was open the French doors in the living room and walk out onto the deck. She looked over the rail at a lone fly fisherman a short distance down the river. Unlike the first time she stood there, Quinn's thoughts did not turn to Patrick. Instead she enjoyed the view of the river and wondered if the fisherman was having any luck.

She turned, walked back into the living room, and put Ricky Nelson's *Greatest Hits* into the CD player.

Singing along to the familiar tunes, she danced into the kitchen and opened the refrigerator.

"Yes!" She made a triumphant gesture. There was still one diet root beer left on the bottom shelf. She grabbed the can, reached for the phone on the wall, and punched in Linda Lou's number.

"Hi. I'm back," she said. "Thanks for spiffying up the place. Was everything okay while I was gone?"

"Oh, sure. I checked a couple of times and everything was fine. But I've got some big news for you."

"What's up?" Quinn popped open the can and took a sip.

"Come over for dinner and I'll tell you the whole story. Be here at six."

Quinn pulled her SUV into Linda Lou's driveway at five-thirty. The small Cape Cod bungalow looked out of place nestled among the faux adobe homes on the block. Hanging next to the front door was a *ristra* of red chiles. She padded to the front door and rang the bell.

"You're early," Linda Lou said opening the door.

"I had to run a few errands in town and I got done ahead of schedule."

Linda Lou studied Quinn's face. "No, you didn't. You just couldn't wait to hear my news."

"You caught me," she answered with a slight blush.

"Come on in and have a seat in the dining room. Dinner is about ready."

Linda Lou placed taco fixings on the table and handed Quinn a diet root beer. Then she sat down and folded her hands on top of the table.

Quinn leaned forward and stared at her. "Well?"

"I guess you haven't checked your mail yet. If you had, you'd know what I was talking about. I got the news three days ago." She sipped on her iced tea.

"Jeez, Linda Lou. Out with it."

"Who would have guessed? Bunny ran off and married her mysterious new boyfriend. The announcement said she married Jim Davis two weeks ago in Las Vegas."

"Jim Davis? Do I know him?"

"It's Davis. You know, from the bar."

Quinn gagged on her taco and took a quick gulp of soda to wash it down. "He was wearing a wedding ring. I thought he was already married," she said.

"Oh, for heaven's sake, no. He's been a widower for ten years. Just couldn't bear to take off his ring. He and Millie were married right out of high school, childhood sweethearts and all that."

"Bunny married ... and to Davis."

"You ain't kidding, sweetie. Remember how she skirted the issue when we asked about her boyfriend at the UFO site. Nobody had any idea those two were dating." Linda Lou placed a tomato slice in her taco and added green chile sauce before munching down.

"And she was always too busy to have lunch. They must have been meeting clandestinely at noon someplace," Quinn added.

"I bet they were. Well, maybe now that she's married, we'll actually see more of her."

Quinn's expression turned serious. "I feel bad. I had all kinds of nasty thoughts about Davis." She grabbed another taco shell and began stuffing it with filling.

"Nasty thoughts?"

"I thought he was a married man trying to pick up women behind his wife's back. I guess I transferred some of my anger about Patrick to Davis." She sprinkled lettuce and cheese on her taco and took a bite.

"He was just a good old boy trying to find a good old girl." Linda Lou seemed wistful for a moment and sighed.

"Guess he found one. Have you talked to her since you got the announcement?"

"I called a couple of times, but no one answered," Linda Lou said.

"I suppose they were *otherwise* occupied." Quinn raised her eyebrows.

The two women snickered.

Linda Lou took a few bites of her taco and leaned back in her chair. "How was your trip?"

"It was the best birthday present ever. Paris was wonderful and it was fun to spend time with Eddy. We used to do everything together." Quinn finished her diet root beer. "Have you got anymore of these?"

"Sure, be right back." Linda Lou headed for the kitchen. She returned carrying a soda can and set it in front of Quinn. With her other hand she slid a five dollar bill onto the table.

"What's this for?"

"You won the bet. Two days after you left for Paris, Hugo asked me out."

Quinn grinned and stuffed the money into the pocket of her jeans. "You went, didn't you?"

"Of course, a girl can't turn down her boss. We went to a jazz concert." She sat and helped herself to another taco.

"How did it go?"

"The concert was great."

"You know what I mean." Quinn tipped her chin down and looked straight into her friend's eyes.

"He told me he'd wanted to ask me out for a long time but was afraid I'd turn him down. Then he admitted he'd invented the story about needing another secretary. He did it so he could spend time with me and butter me up before asking for a date."

"Wow, that's quite an admission from a man."

"And he said I didn't have to worry about my job either. He said I could have it as long as I wanted because I really am a great secretary. Then he kissed me and my stomach did a flip-flop."

"So, I guess you're going out again?" Quinn smiled.

"We've been out every night since." Linda Lou fluffed out one side of her hairdo. "And by the way, when are you going to start dating again? You're not getting any younger. You need to find a man of your own and stop obsessing over Sam Maxwell."

"What's this about me finding a man? And by the way, I'm over Sam Maxwell. A few weeks ago you weren't the least bit interested in finding a man for yourself, and now you're saying I need to find one."

"Well, I hate to admit it, but I was wrong," Linda Lou said. "And I think I know just the man for you."

The message light on the phone was blinking when Quinn got home. She pushed the playback button.

"Mom, you've got to get here soon." Megan sounded exhausted. "Please call me."

Quinn hit the auto-dial.

Megan answered on the second ring. "Oh, Mom. Things are getting out of control. I thought I could manage all this by myself, but it's too much!"

"Calm down, honey," Quinn said cradling the phone between her head and shoulder. "What's the problem?"

"Everything! I have to work, and all this wedding stuff takes so much time, and Perry is being a jerk. I really need you here *now.*"

"What's Perry done? Whatever it is, you don't have to put up with it!" Quinn could feel her own anxiety rising.

"Oh, he just isn't any help. Whenever I ask him to do something, like help with the invitations, he tells me I can do a better job. Then he goes and watches some game on television."

"How about his mother, can't she help with a few things?"

"She's offered. But Mom, I need you. You always know what needs to get done and the right way to do it."

"I'll see if I can get there by next weekend, but I've got some things I need to do around here first."

"Thanks, Mom. You always save my butt. How was your birthday? Or should I say, how was Paris?"

"You know about Paris?"

"Eddy called and told me she was going to take you but that the whole thing was supposed to be a surprise."

"*C'est magnifique.* She really showed me the sights. We even stayed at the Ritz."

"When you get here, you'll have to tell me all about the trip and everything you've been up to since we've seen each other."

"Of course," Quinn lied.

Quinn parked on the street in front of Linda Lou's house and drummed her fingers on the steering wheel.

Blind dates can be a curse. Why did I agree to this one?

She stared out the window of her Tahoe at the vehicle parked in Linda Lou's driveway. The shiny, black pickup almost glowed.

It must belong to Hugo's friend, Bart Mason. Bart Mason, now there's a manly name to go with his manly vehicle. I can just see him—tall, studly, wearing a black shirt and black jeans to match his truck.

Maybe I shouldn't go in. After all, I have a daughter in Philadelphia who needs me. I should be home packing and not messing with a blind date. Besides, blind dates never worked out when I was young and this one probably won't either. Still, Linda Lou is a good friend and she went to a lot of trouble to arrange this little get together on short notice.

Quinn opened the driver's door and jumped out. Static cling caused her skirt to hike halfway up her slip. She pulled her skirt into place, grabbed her purse off the center console, stiffened her back, and walked to the front door.

"You're right on time," Linda Lou said. "Come on in."

Hugo and Bart were in the dining room talking about baseball and drinking cans of Bud Light. Bart stood about six feet tall, wore a black silk T-shirt, tan slacks, and black loafers.

Not exactly what I'd call a stud muffin—more like a well-dressed nerd. Oh, maybe he'll be okay.

After brief introductions, Linda Lou announced dinner was ready and everyone sat around the dining room table.

Bart looked at the table and moved his fork from between the knife and spoon to the other side of his plate.

Linda Lou's eyes narrowed.

"Mom always sets the table with the fork on the left," Bart said in a self-satisfied tone.

Quinn saw Linda Lou's eyes darken. Whether or not "mom" was correct in the way she arranged the place settings, Quinn thought it presumptuous for Bart to say such a thing.

"Bart is a mortgage banker," Hugo told Quinn in an obvious attempt to shift attention away from how the table was set. "We've known each other since the third grade."

"How nice," Quinn said.

The rest of the dinner was pleasant enough. Linda Lou's roast was perfectly browned yet moist and the gravy was delicious. The glazed carrots were yummy and Quinn asked for the recipe. Dessert was a homemade peach pie.

After the meal, the men carried the dishes to the kitchen. Linda Lou and Quinn put up the leftovers. Hugo stood next to the counter while Bart rinsed the dishes and neatly piled them into three stacks based on size. All the silverware was placed in one heap, except for the cooking utensils which Bart arranged separately. He lined the glasses up in a straight row next to the silverware.

"I keep saying I'm going to get a dishwasher, but I don't know where I'd put it in this little kitchen," Linda Lou said.

"I'll help—we'll get these done in no time." Quinn took the dishtowel off the hook at the end of counter and prepared to dry. Linda Lou filled the sink and put the plates into the dishwater.

"You're not going to wash the plates first, are you?" Bart peered over Linda Lou's shoulder.

"That's what I had in mind," she replied her voice tinged with ice.

"Mom always washes the glasses and silverware first. You know, because they touch the mouth," Bart said hovering behind Linda Lou.

"Come on, Bart. Let's go out in the living room and let the girls finish up in here," Hugo said. He grabbed a couple beers from the fridge and led Bart away by the arm.

Linda Lou put her hands on her hips and frowned. "I've known Bart for years and never realized he was such a mama's boy or that he could be so irritating. Guess I'll have to find someone else for you."

Quinn put on her best fake smile. *Thank goodness, I'm going to Philadelphia!*

Chapter Twenty

Perry groaned as he lugged Quinn's suitcases over the threshold of Megan's apartment. "I guess it's true what they say, women don't know how to travel light."

"You know how it is," Quinn scolded raising her eyebrows and pointing upward with her index finger. "A woman's got to make sure she has the right dress for every occasion. I brought three choices for the wedding. I'll let Megan decide which one is best." She paused and smiled weakly. "And I brought two more for the rehearsal dinner, and a couple of additional ones just in case I need them."

"Females," Perry muttered. He set the luggage down and stretched his back.

"I have the guest bedroom ready for you, Mom." Megan led the way through the living room and down a short hall to a cozy room decorated in shades of blue with white accents. A double wedding ring quilt covered the bed and a large window overlooked the city.

"Is that the quilt your grandmother gave you for graduation?" Quinn asked.

"Yes, doesn't it match perfectly in here?" Megan smiled.

"It looks lovely, but I think she meant for you to save it until after you're married."

"Well, you're the first one to use it, and I'm almost married." Megan straightened her posture and placed her hands on her hips. "So, I don't think she'd mind."

"I know she would be very happy for you, honey." Quinn walked to the window and gazed outside. "What a great view."

"That's the reason I decided to live on the fifth floor. You should see it at night, the lights are fantastic."

Perry brought the suitcases into the bedroom. "Good thing she picked a place with an elevator," he said. "We're living here after the wedding and there's no way I want to walk up and down four flights of stairs every day. Where do you want these?" he asked Quinn.

"Put them on the bed," Megan snapped before Quinn could answer. "So it's easy for Mom to unpack."

"How thoughtful of you, honey," Quinn said. "But I could have managed myself."

Megan opened the closet door. "There are plenty of hangers." She turned and walked to the chest against the opposite wall. "And I've cleaned out a couple of drawers in here."

"Maybe your mom would like something to eat," Perry suggested.

"Oh, gosh. What was I thinking? Make yourself comfortable out in the living room, Mom. I'll fix a snack. You must be hungry from your trip."

"Actually, I grabbed a snack on the plane but I could use a cool drink to tide me over until dinner."

"I'll get it," Perry said and hurried out of the room ahead of them.

"He really likes you, Mom."

"What's not to like?" Secretly pleased she grinned and followed Megan to the living room. She settled into the comfy leather sofa across from a large screen television hanging on the wall.

"It's Perry's," Megan said. "He decided to put it here since the wedding is so close."

"It certainly is big. No wonder he wants to watch sports instead of working on wedding stuff."

Perry returned carrying a frost-covered mug. "Megan says this is your favorite—diet root beer." He handed the drink to Quinn and then plopped beside her.

"Thanks." Quinn took a sip. "I usually don't get a frosty mug, this is great."

Perry leaned back and clasped his hands behind his head. "You know, my Uncle Mack really is a great guy. It's too bad you missed each other in LA. I think you would be a perfect match. He's coming to the wedding. How about I set you up on a date?"

"That would be ..." Quinn stopped when she saw Megan glare at Perry.

"Mother isn't ready to date yet. It's too soon. Isn't it, Mom?"

Quinn swallowed. "Well ..."

"In the kitchen, Megan," Perry demanded. He frowned at her, got up from the sofa, and motioned for her to follow him around the corner.

The open wall between the living room and the dining area made it easy for Quinn to overhear their conversation in the kitchen even though they kept their voices low.

"Don't you think a year of mourning is enough?" Perry asked.

"They were married twenty-six years. It takes a while to get over that. I just can't see her with another man."

"That's the problem—*you* can't see her with someone else. What about how your mother feels?"

Quinn squirmed. *I hope this doesn't turn into a fight.*

"Don't hassle me, Perry." Megan's voice took a firm tone. "Trust me. I know I'm right about this."

Quinn could almost see her daughter's blue eyes flash in defiance. *Poor Perry.*

"We'll talk later," he said as the two came back into the living room.

"Is everything okay?" Quinn asked.

"Peachy," Perry said and glanced at Megan. "I just didn't want to give your daughter a passionate kiss in front of her mom."

Megan blushed.

"How about a game of Scrabble?" Quinn asked.

Sunday they attended services at the historic Methodist church where the wedding was to take place.

"Isn't it beautiful? It's over two hundred years old. I've always dreamed of being married in a church like this," Megan said as they approached the entrance.

The Perpendicular Gothic style of the building with its red brick and ornate granite arches was unlike any church Quinn had attended. Inside, the stained glass windows cast rainbow hues over the center aisle.

"A sign," Quinn whispered.

"This looks like a good spot," Perry said and helped Quinn and Megan into a pew near the center of the sanctuary.

Quinn was surprised to see a middle-aged female pastor approach the pulpit to deliver the sermon. *Don't be such a sexist,* she told herself.

The minister gave an eloquent, uplifting sermon calling for tolerance in the face of differences.

"She's wonderful, isn't she?" Megan whispered in Quinn's ear at the close of the sermon.

"Yes, honey. She's very inspiring." Quinn gave Megan a little hug. As they left the church, she reflected on Megan's desire to meddle in her life and decided to be more understanding. After all, her father was dead. Naturally, she'd be protective of her mother.

Megan climbed into the back seat of Perry's Mercedes. "You ride up front again, Mom. I don't want you to have to struggle getting in and out."

My Lord! She really does think I'm helpless. Quinn smiled through clenched teeth.

Perry held the door for her then climbed into the driver's seat. She clicked her seatbelt in place, and adjusted her skirt to cover her knees.

Megan tapped her on the shoulder and continued talking. "Isn't it great that the pastor is a woman? Gosh, being married by a woman—who would have guessed? I really like her. Didn't you get a special feeling when she greeted you after the service?"

"She certainly seems likeable and the church is perfect. It has such a dignified air about it."

"We found it six months ago and have been attending regularly," Perry said and pulled out of the parking lot. "Look at the battlement atop the bell tower. It's hard to imagine all the work it took to carve such a masterpiece."

Quinn gazed at it through the window as they drove away. "It's magnificent."

A few blocks later, she ran her hand along the edge of the plush front seat. "This is such a comfortable car. Have you had it long?"

"It belongs to my mother. I borrowed it until after the wedding. I drive ... I should say my mom is now driving my old blue Corvette. She insisted I drive you around in a decent car while you're here."

"That was very kind of her." Quinn thought about Eddy's love of Corvettes. Perry was a man after Eddy's own heart. She knew they would get along great.

"Perry's mom is a wonderful person. You'll get to meet her next weekend. They are having us over for dinner."

Quinn spent the first part of the week on the phone double-checking wedding details. In the evenings she went over her notes with Megan. Perry added his two cents once in a while but most nights he stretched out on the living room couch and watched television.

When Megan came home Thursday night, Quinn announced, "Tomorrow after work, we need to go to the hotel. We have to sample the menu for the reception."

"But Mom, I've already taken care of that." Megan kicked off her high heels and plodded into the kitchen. "Perry and I sampled the food and it was delicious."

"If I'm paying for it, I want to taste it," Quinn called from the dining room table. "And I want to see the reception room too. So, I've made us an appointment."

Megan sighed and shrugged her shoulders. "Okay, Mom. But remember we can't go checking on anything Saturday because we're going to the North's."

"This will be easy for everyone to find," Quinn said as Megan pulled to a stop near the front entrance of the hotel.

"And there is plenty of parking," Megan added. "Come on, let's get this over with."

The special event manager served Quinn the entire menu. The salmon with dill sauce had just the right texture and tasted delectable. Everything else Megan and Perry had selected was excellent.

I should have trusted Megan's word on the food. Still, I feel better having tasted it myself.

Gilded flower reliefs and vertical mirrors lined the walls of the reception room. There was a large stage for a band and plenty of space for dancing.

"Wow, the room is so elegant," Quinn said and turned toward Megan. "I know you must think I've been a pain lately—but you wanted me to help. I'm just trying to make sure your day is perfect." She fidgeted with her purple Versace handbag.

"I know, Mom. You've been a lifesaver."

Quinn opened the bedroom closet and moved the hangers back and forth. "What should I wear?" she asked Megan.

"Gosh, Mom. You've got half a dress shop in there. Just pick something."

"How about this?" She pulled out a wrap dress with pink flowers and held it in front of herself. "Do you think this is suitable for meeting your future in-laws?"

"Perfect. But hurry, we need to get there around three." Megan hustled back to the living room where Perry was waiting.

Quinn slipped into the dress and added her pearls. She dumped the contents for her handbag into a spacious straw purse with pink leather trim and put on pink ballet flats with little rhinestones decorating the toes. After touching up her makeup, she checked her watch.

"Five minutes flat, not bad." She trotted out to join the kids.

An hour's drive later, they arrived at the home of the North's. The gray English Tudor house was trimmed in white and sat nestled among large oak trees. A variety of manicured shrubs lined the exterior of the house. A narrow brick path stretched across the front lawn leading to a small vine-covered porch where an ornate wrought iron chair sat next to the front door. To Quinn, the whole scene seemed to say, "Come join us." She wondered if the people inside would be as welcoming.

"We're here," Perry called as he opened the front door.

Mrs. North rushed into the entry hall. "At last, I've missed seeing you two," she said hugging Megan and Perry. "But I know you've been busy with all the wedding planning." She disengaged herself, turned to Quinn and offered her hand, "I'm so glad to finally meet you."

"Nice to meet you, also," Quinn replied. There was a gentle elegance in the tall blonde's delicate features and the way she moved. Quinn liked her right away.

"It's such a lovely afternoon, let's go out on the back porch and have some lemonade. It will give us a chance to visit," Mrs.

North said to Quinn. "Perry, you show her the way and Megan and I will bring out the drinks."

Perry's dad was snoozing in a high-backed wicker armchair when Quinn and Perry came out onto the porch.

"I don't want to wake him," she whispered.

"Don't worry, I was just resting my eyes," Mr. North said. He rose from his chair and greeted Quinn.

She was surprised by the man's height. He was almost a full head taller than Perry. His white-streaked, gray hair was combed straight back from his face and fell gently over the top of his ears. Faint smile lines ran down the sides of his face.

"Please, have a seat." He motioned to a line of wicker chairs on the porch.

Quinn sat beside a giant potted Boston fern. On the opposite side of the fern, a marble slab supported by short Doric columns held various plants.

"What a lovely coleus plant," she said gesturing toward a large ceramic vase on the edge of the porch.

"Oh, is that what it's called?" Mr. North smiled. "Plants are my wife's thing. I just enjoy their ambience."

Mrs. North and Megan emerged from the house carrying a tray of glasses and a huge pitcher of lemonade with citrus slices floating inside. Megan passed out the glasses and Mrs. North poured.

After a few sips, Mr. North looked at Quinn. "Perry tells me you missed meeting Mack in LA. That's too bad, he's a great guy."

"He's one of our oldest and dearest friends. We've known him since our college days," Mrs. North added. "I'm so pleased he's coming for the wedding."

"Say, Quinn, the two of you might hit it off," Perry's dad said. He looked up as if in thought. "Be sure to save him a dance."

"I'll do that," she said.

Perry smiled and put his hand on Megan's shoulder. She frowned at her mother but didn't say a word.

Cat got your tongue, Megan?

Chapter Twenty-One

"Eddy! I'm so glad you could come for the wedding," Megan squealed spotting her mother's best friend sitting on a couch in the hotel lobby.

"A herd of wild buffalo couldn't have kept me away, kid." Eddy rose and kissed her on the cheek.

"I'm sorry I couldn't meet you at the airport," Megan said. "You know how it is with work. Since I'll be gone for two weeks on my honeymoon, I don't want to rock the boat too much. I came as soon as I got off."

Eddy put her arm around Megan's shoulder. "Not to worry. I've been to Philly many times and had no trouble finding the hotel."

"Mom told you the reception is going to be here, didn't she? She's waiting at my place. It's not too far. We'll pick her up and head for the rehearsal."

"Good, you can tell me all about Perry on our way. Your mom said he passed the muster with her."

Megan led the way out of the lobby. "Yeah, I think she really likes him. The two of them have a mutual admiration society going."

"That's good, isn't it?" Eddy asked as they ambled the short distance to Megan's white Ford.

Megan leaned against the car. "I guess it's a good thing." She narrowed her eyes, and stuck out her lower lip. "Unless they decide to gang up on me."

"That look reminds me of when you were three and Rick wouldn't let you play with his dump truck. Is he here yet?"

"Nope. He won't get here until tomorrow."

"Too bad." Eddy climbed into the passenger seat.

"He said he didn't need to rehearse. He's giving me away, you know," Megan got into the car and turned on the ignition.

"He always said he wanted to get rid of you," Eddy chuckled. "Now, let's go get your mom and you can tell me all about this lawyer of yours on the way."

Megan pulled out into traffic and headed for her apartment.

Quinn, Eddy, and Megan arrived at the church to find everyone else waiting for them.

"We got here as fast as we could," Megan told Perry.

He slipped his arm around her waist. "I just arrived myself."

"Eddy, this is Perry," Megan beamed.

"So I guessed." She gave Megan a wink.

"Let me introduce you to everyone," he offered and led Eddy around the room. A petite brunette with a friendly smile sat in a pew near the back of the sanctuary. "This is my sister, Paige. Mom had a thing for *P's* when she named us. Oh, here comes my niece, Olivia." He bent onto one knee.

A bubbly five year old ran up and hugged his neck. He stood lifting her with him.

"Uncle Perry, do you have my five dollars?"

"Five dollars?" He looked puzzled.

"The five dollars I get if I'm good."

"Oh, you mean *this* five dollars." He pulled a crisp bill from the pocket of his pants.

Her eyes widened and she grabbed for the money.

"Not so fast." He jerked the five dollar bill out of her reach. "This is for after the wedding."

"Okay," she said and kissed his cheek. "Put me down." She bounded off as soon as her feet hit the ground.

"Olivia's the flower girl," Paige told Eddy. "She's been rehearsing in our living room for the last month. I just hope she doesn't get too dramatic throwing the petals."

"She'll be perfect," Perry said.

The minister gathered all the participants for the rehearsal. Mr. North stood in for Rick and walked Megan down the aisle. Olivia threw the flower petals on cue and then scurried up the aisle stuffing them back into her basket.

"Olivia," Paige called. "Wait until we are finished to do that. Come back down here."

The little girl frowned and walked to the front of the church. Her lower lip trembled as she looked at Perry.

"Don't worry, you haven't lost your five dollars," he said.

After the rehearsal, everyone headed for a local Italian restaurant where Perry's parents hosted dinner.

Eddy sat at a table with Quinn and Mr. and Mrs. North. "You can sure tell those two are related," she said looking at Olivia perched on a chair next to Perry. "They have the same green eyes."

Perry's mother smiled. "And the same streak of orneriness."

Olivia only nibbled at her spaghetti dinner. Yet, she managed to finagle Perry into getting her two bowls of spumoni ice cream before her parents whisked her away for bed.

"Another round of wine," Mr. North told the mustachioed waiter who quickly obliged.

"I was sure Mack would be here by now," Perry said moving to an empty chair next to his mother. "I wanted him to meet Megan and Quinn before the wedding."

"You know he'll be here as soon as he can. Maybe his flight got delayed." She gave him a hug. "Go, enjoy yourself."

The next morning the doorbell rang three times in quick succession before Quinn opened the door.

"That was some rehearsal dinner last night," Eddy said leaning red-eyed against the doorjamb of Megan's apartment. "My head still hurts from all the wine Perry's dad kept ordering."

"Come on in. Breakfast is ready."

Eddy followed her to the dining room and put her purse on the floor next to the table. Quinn brought pancakes, scrambled eggs and orange juice from the kitchen and set out two place settings.

"Shit." Eddy shielded her eyes from the bright sunlight streaming through the window. "I thought it was supposed to rain this morning."

"Guess not. Why don't you move to the other side of the table so the sun won't be in your eyes?" Quinn rearranged the plates. "Sorry, I don't have a hangover cure handy."

"I'll survive. That's much better," Eddy said sliding into the chair. She rubbed her temples. "Too bad Uncle Mack didn't make it to the rehearsal. Perry seemed bummed when he didn't arrive."

"He's been saying he wants to set me up with Mack ever since we were all in LA." Quinn sat, reached for the bowl of eggs, and scooped a large portion onto her plate. "But Megan keeps putting the kibosh on it."

"Maybe you should give this Uncle Mack a try. Everyone seems to like him."

"I don't know about blind dates." She rubbed her hands on the sides of her slacks. "The last one I had was a doozy."

Eddy drank half a glass of juice. "Has Megan taken you to Pat's or Geno's yet?"

"Are they restaurants?"

"Not quite. Just a couple of little take-out joints, but they have the best cheese steaks in town. Omigod, you mean you've been in Philly for almost a month and you haven't been to either place? They're famous."

"Well, I've never heard of them." Quinn forked two pancakes onto her plate and looked up at her friend. "I can't believe you. You just walked in the door, we haven't even finished breakfast, and already you're talking about more food."

"That's it. We're going to South Philly for lunch." She poured several globs of maple syrup onto her hotcakes.

"But …"

"No buts about it. We'll take my rental car. I know how to get there. End of discussion." Eddy stuffed a double-decker bite of pancake into her mouth.

"Well, I guess that settles that." She poured more juice into Eddy's glass. "What do you think of Perry and his family?"

"His dad sure can down the wine and that little Olivia is a real pip, isn't she?"

"You said it."

"Perry looks like a nerd in those glasses but I can see there's a wild streak in that boy."

"I knew you'd like him." Quinn got a warm feeling inside.

At half past noon, Eddy parked a few blocks away from the X-shaped intersection of Ninth and Passyunk where Pat's and Geno's are located.

"It's hard to find parking around here especially this time of day," Eddy said. "Besides we can both use the exercise and it will be worth the walk."

Quinn gawked at all the people lined up outside the two establishments.

"You decide. Which place is it?" Eddy asked.

"Jeez, I don't know. Let's try Pat's."

"Want yours w'd or w'd out?" Eddy said in a South Philly accent. "That's with or without onions for us tourists."

"With."

"Wait here, the ordering is fast and furious. I'll be right back."

Quinn watched Eddy scramble into the line just outside the shop. She glanced at the storm clouds gathering overhead and wished she had an umbrella. In a few minutes, Eddy returned carrying two sandwiches and two drinks.

"Where do we eat?" Quinn asked looking around for a place to sit.

"Right here. Set your soda on the ground and start eating. But be sure to stoop over or you'll drip juice on yourself."

Quinn opened the paper wrapper, bent over a little and took a bite. Juice ran down the front of her white blouse. "Crap, look at me!" She watched the greasy liquid sink into the fabric.

"You're such a klutz. I warned you." Eddy opened her handbag and pulled out a stain removal pen. "Here, give this a try," she said handing it to Quinn.

"It seems to be working," Quinn said as she pressed and dabbed the pen against her blouse.

"You might not be this lucky at the wedding tomorrow. You'd better stash one of your extra dresses in my room at the hotel—in case of an emergency."

Quinn grimaced. "Maybe you're right." She handed the pen back to Eddy and took another bite of her sandwich. "You know, this really is good."

"I told you. If you come to Philly, you've got to come here."

Thunder clapped overhead.

"We'd better hurry. It looks like we are in for rain after all," Quinn said.

They gobbled down their sandwiches and made a mad dash for the car.

Chapter Twenty-Two

Quinn sat alone in the front pew waiting for the wedding to begin. She turned and squinted looking up the aisle in a vain attempt to see Megan and Rick at the rear of the church.

Megan will be missing Patrick today.

She remembered how he joked about the old television commercial where the father hands his daughter a Life Saver candy just before they head down the aisle. The whole family knew he planned do the same thing on Megan's special day.

It would have put Megan at ease. She felt a speck of softness in her heart for Patrick, but only for a moment.

She shifted her glance to Perry's mother and father seated across the aisle. Dressed in a champagne silk suit, Mrs. North looked like a picture out of *Vogue*. Her husband held her hand and appeared dignified and calm. But Quinn noticed he was nervously tapping his right foot on the floor.

A gentle poke on Quinn's shoulder roused her from her thoughts.

"Have you met him yet?" Eddy whispered from the pew behind her.

"Who?"

"The mysterious Uncle Mack?"

"I don't think he's arrived, at least I haven't met him." Pipe organ music interrupted their conversation.

Perry and his groomsmen, looking a bit uneasy in their black tuxedos, slipped in from a side entrance and stood in front of the alter. Everyone turned and looked up the center aisle of the church.

The bridesmaids in Grecian floor-length gowns started down the aisle. The young women seemed to glow as light streamed through the stained glass windows and blended with the pale pink of their dresses. Following close behind with a broad smile, Olivia almost skipped down the aisle tossing pink rose petals from her basket.

Quinn cast a brief look at her future son-in-law. Perry's right hand was shaking and she saw him clutch the side of his trousers. He drew in a quick breath as if steadying himself.

Like father, like son.

The wedding march resounded throughout the sanctuary. The congregation stood and turned toward the back of the church.

Quinn strained to see up the aisle but her view was blocked by rows of guests. She stretched her body beyond the end of the pew. Thrown off balance, her left heel slipped off the edge of her three-inch slides and she started to fall.

In a flash, Eddy reached over the pew and grabbed her upper arm preventing an embarrassing head dive.

"Thanks," Quinn sighed and grinned at her friend. *That's all I would have needed—another shoe disaster.* She repositioned her foot in the shoe and straightened back up. *Thank goodness the congregation wasn't looking this direction.*

Megan came into view and a tear ran down Quinn's cheek. *She's never looked more beautiful.*

Confident and serene Megan strolled down the aisle on her brother's arm. Her upswept raven hair drew attention to her vibrant blue eyes. The radiance of her complexion was accentuated by the beaded bodice of her Vera Wang gown. She smiled graciously at individual guests as she and Rick made their way to the front of the church.

Quinn sniffled and Eddy handed her a handkerchief.

The minister greeted the congregation and presented a short message on the sanctity of marriage. "Who gives this woman?" she asked.

"I do," Rick declared and then slipped into the front pew beside his mother.

Perry and Megan stood facing each other as the vows preceded.

"I take thee," Megan began, and then stopped. She looked down, took a deep breath, and gazed up at Perry. "I take thee," she stopped again. Her face turned bright crimson and she bit her lower lip.

Quinn's stomach knotted and she feared a runaway bride scenario. Perry's parents appeared to be holding their breath.

Eleven ... twelve ... thirteen seconds ticked away, fourteen ... fifteen.

Tiny Olivia took three deliberate steps toward Megan. Her little hand reached up and tugged on the side of the bridal gown. A smile crossed her face and her elfin voice declared with great gusto, "Megan, it's Uncle Perry."

Startled out of her stupor, Megan bent down and whispered, "Thank you."

Quinn's heart began to beat again. Audible sighs of relief and laughter echoed in the sanctuary.

Megan began anew, "I take thee, Perry North."

He gave her a wink.

Soon the newly married couple strode up the aisle to the sound of church bells.

Rick stood and took his mother's arm. "Olivia not only earned her five dollars, but I think she deserves an extra piece of cake at the reception," he whispered in Quinn's ear.

One hundred and thirty guests chatted at tables decorated with crystal vases overflowing with pink roses. The young adults of the wedding party occupied a long rectangular table near the orchestra.

"May your marriage be long and happy," Rick toasted as the guests raised their wineglasses to the newly married couple.

Eddy and Quinn were seated at the parents' table not far from the wedding party.

"It's too bad you don't have many relatives left to help celebrate," Eddy said to Quinn.

"My mother would have loved seeing the wedding. Thank goodness for Aunt Martha and Aunt Sally. It's like a touch of Mom when they're around."

"I see Patrick's family came out in force," Eddy said looking over the crowd.

"Most of them have no idea of the circumstances surrounding Patrick's death. As far as I'm concerned, it's better that way. Still, I feel a little uncomfortable with his sister here. She's never liked me."

"Don't give that—you know what—another thought." Eddy turned to Mr. North, "Is Uncle Mack here?"

Quinn flashed the evil eye and gave her a swift kick under the table.

"I haven't seen him. He called late last night to say his flight had been cancelled and he was going to try to fly in this morning," Mr. North said.

"Since he missed the wedding, Perry will be really disappointed if he doesn't get to the reception," Mrs. North added.

"He wasn't going to be able to stay long as it was. He has a meeting in New York." Mr. North gave his wife a weak smile.

"Perry has told Quinn so much about Mack, she's dying to meet him," Eddy smiled as she spoke.

Quinn's face reddened. "What Eddy meant to say was it's always nice to meet people who mean so much to those you care about." She took a sip of her wine and tried to look unruffled.

Mr. North glanced around the room. "There's his business partner by the punch bowl, so Mack can't be too far away."

Eddy spied him first and gasped. "Look who it is," she whispered to Quinn.

Not wanting to appear obvious, Quinn raised her glass and took another sip before turning to get a clear view of the man.

"It's Cigar Man!" The glass slipped from her fingers splashing wine down the front of her dress and onto her lap.

"Shit! Look at you, you're a mess." Eddy snatched her arm and jerked her out of the chair. "Come on, you need to change. You can't stay at your daughter's wedding looking like this."

Quinn smiled weakly at Perry's parents. "Excuse us. We'll be back in a few minutes."

"It's a good thing you stashed that extra dress in my room," Eddy said. They scurried toward the exit taking care to avoid the punch bowl area.

Patrick's sister, Rosemary, stepped out from between the tables blocking their way with her ample figure.

"Quinn darling, it's so good to see you," she cooed with insincerity. "My goodness, whatever happened to your dress."

"Just a little spill. I'm on my way to change."

Rosemary did not move. "It was such a lovely wedding. Of course, *our* family would have preferred a Catholic ceremony. But then, you never were one to take religion seriously."

Quinn felt her temperature rising. Rosemary had not spoken a civil word to her in twenty-six years and she did not have a clue why.

"Megan was raised in the Methodist church, so I hardly think a Catholic wedding would have been appropriate," Quinn snapped.

Out of nowhere came a familiar voice.

"Rosemary dear, I haven't seen you in ages. My, the years have certainly been kind to you." Aunt Martha wedged herself between the two women. "Come, have a glass of wine with Sally and me. You remember Quinn's Aunt Sally, don't you?" She took Rosemary's arm and swiftly moved her out of Quinn's path.

"Just one more word out of Rosemary and I swear I would have smacked that bitch," Quinn hissed.

"No, you wouldn't have. You're too nice." Eddy pulled Quinn toward the north exit of the ballroom.

"Well, thank goodness for Aunt Martha, she's such a diplomat," Quinn said.

"On second thought, I think I should stay here while you change." Eddy grinned.

"Oh, I forgot—Cigar Man. Or, are we calling him Marty now?" Quinn chided. "I don't care what you say. You've been dying to see him since Paris."

"Hurry," Eddy told her, "I might need your help."

"I wouldn't bet on it." Quinn chuckled and left the room.

Eddy wandered over to an empty table where she had a clear view of the goings-on. She was about to sashay over to Marty's table when a tall, red-haired man with glasses strode into the room and headed toward Marty. The two men shook hand and began talking.

I wonder who he is.

She listened intently but could only make out snippets of their conversation including "my godson," and "where is the young buck?"

Godson, he must be Uncle Mack.

The man's eyes searched the room. He made his way across the dance floor, and found Perry and his mother as the music ended.

Eddy skulked after him and sat at the edge of the dance floor. *I've got to check him out for Quinn.*

"Ellen, you look stunning," he said. "I can't believe Pete let you out of his sight."

"Mack, you're such a flatterer. I'm so glad you finally got here." She gave him a kiss on his cheek. "By the way, I love your hair," she giggled.

"Well, young man," Mack said. "Where's Megan? Don't you think it's about time I get to know her?"

"She said she was going to find her great-aunts. There she is." He pointed to a table halfway across the room.

"See you later, lady killer," Ellen teased Mack and wandered back to her table.

At a safe distance, Eddy followed Perry and Mack as they walked toward Megan.

"Honey, I'd like you to meet my Uncle Mack," Perry said and kissed Megan on the back of her neck.

She got up from her chair and turned to face them. "Ah ... oh, I mean, hello. It's nice to finally meet you," she blushed before lowering her eyes and offering her hand to Mack.

"The pleasure is mine." He looked at the two gray-haired women and the one obviously dyed redhead who sat between them. "And, these fine women are?"

Megan introduced them.

"Haven't we met? You look very familiar," Rosemary said giving Mack the once-over.

"Not that I recall. But I could be mistaken." He turned to Perry. "Let's find your parents."

Perry grabbed Megan's hand and pulled her along beside him.

"I'd really like you to meet my mom," Megan told Mack as they walked.

Perry did a double take.

A few minutes had turned into forty-five by the time Quinn changed into a different dress, touched up her makeup, and returned to the ballroom.

Megan greeted her mother with a scowl. "Where have you been? You missed him."

"I had to change my clothes. Missed who?"

"Mack. Perry's Uncle Mack was here and you missed him." Megan looked dejected.

"I thought you didn't want me to meet him."

"I didn't. But Mom, you should have seen him—he's so hot. He has the bluest eyes and this great red hair. One look at him could melt ice. If it weren't for Perry, I'd go for him myself even if he is an old guy."

"He must really be something."

"And he is *so* nice. I have the strangest feeling that I know him, but I can't figure out from where. Aunt Rosemary had the same feeling."

"You know Aunt Rosemary, she'd use any excuse to cozy up to a man. And as for you, I'm sure you think he's great because Perry talks about him so much. It's almost like you already know him."

"Maybe, but he's a real hunk. So, I've changed my mind and you're going to have to meet him."

Eddy waved at Quinn from a few tables away.

"Okay, honey," Quinn told Megan. "I'll make a point of meeting him the next time he's around."

Quinn strolled over and joined Eddy at her table.

"It's about time you got back," Eddy said.

"What are you doing sitting over here. I thought you'd be with Marty. Isn't that him sitting all alone?"

"Yes. But I've been busy keeping an eye on Uncle Mack for you. He just left a few minutes ago. I'll tell you all about him later. Right now I've got some business of my own to conduct.

Eddy sauntered across the room to Marty. Placing her hands on his table, she leaned over giving him a clear view of her cleavage.

"Fancy meeting you here," she said.

He dropped his fork. "Eddy! Where did you come from?"

"I suppose you think I followed you here," she scoffed.

"No, really, what are you doing here?"

"I'm a friend of the bride. And you?"

"Friend of the groom."

Eddy sat beside him. "How do you know Perry?"

"Oh, I've only met the kid a few times. But I've known his parents for ages. Mack introduced us."

"Mack, Mack, Mack. That's all I've heard the last two days. Who is this guy anyway?" Eddy nestled against Marty.

"An old friend and a business partner of mine." He draped his arm over her shoulder.

"I hope he's not an A-hole like that Alastair what's his name."

"Hell, no. Mack's as good as they come. But you're right about Alastair."

"What kind of business are you and Mack in?" She batted her eyelashes.

"My business," he said laughing.

"Oh no, here we go again." She wiggled free of his grip and crossed her arms.

Quinn approached the table. "Is everything okay?"

"We're fine," Eddy said. "Marty, this is my best friend, Quinn. She's the mother of the bride."

"At last, I meet your cohort in crime." Marty stood and shook Quinn's hand.

"What did you mean by that crack—cohort in crime?" Eddy demanded.

"I've seen the two of you together a lot, that's all."

"We've been friends most of our lives," Quinn said.

Eddy cocked her head to one side and raised her eyebrows at Quinn.

"Looks like you two are out of wine," Quinn said taking the hint. "I'll find a waiter and have him bring you another bottle." She headed to the opposite side of the room.

Marty sat back down. "Do you live in Philadelphia?"

"No, I flew in for the wedding. How about you?"

"Flew in, too. I have a room across town." His eyes gleamed as he reached under the table and touched her thigh.

"Now, why would you mention a thing like that?" she scolded as heat built in her loins.

"Just in case," he crooned in her ear.

"In case of what?" She gazed into his eyes and touched his cheek.

His lips brushed hers. "In case your room *isn't* upstairs."

"I'm on the third floor," she whispered.

Marty put his arm around her waist, lifted her out of the chair and pulled her tight against him. "Where's the elevator?"

"We missed you last night. Where'd you disappear to?" Quinn asked Eddy over lunch at the airport. "You didn't get to see the cake cutting or the throwing of the bouquet."

"Apologize to Megan. I had to take care of some business."

"Cigar Man business, no doubt."

"No doubt," Eddy smirked.

"The kids left for Hawaii a couple of hours ago. They're so cute together." Quinn dabbed her eye with the napkin.

Eddy opened her Chanel handbag, pulled out some tissue and handed it to Quinn. "Don't get all weepy on me."

"They're staying at Mack's ranch on the Big Island," Quinn said before blowing her nose.

"What kind of a ranch is it?"

"Cattle, I guess." Regaining her composure, she asked, "Did Marty tell you anything more about Mack last night?"

"No. Honestly, I couldn't get anything out of him at first and then I got distracted. But, he seemed nice enough when I was spying on him."

"Some friend you are." Quinn took a sip of iced tea.

"But I did find out that Marty lives in Southern California, up the coast from me in Pacific Palisades. He's divorced—been married a couple times. He's calling me next week and we're going out to dinner. Maybe I can find out more then." She returned to eating her sandwich.

"I've been thinking, now that I own the house in New Mexico, maybe I should sell the one in California. I was going to keep it because of the kids. Now, I'm undecided. What do you think?" Quinn asked.

"Depends. Do you think you'll ever want to move back?"

"I don't think so. And if I do, I don't want to live in a house that reminds me of Patrick."

"You can always stay with me. I have plenty of room."

"I'm going back to New Mexico tomorrow, but I think I'll go to California in August and put it up for sale," Quinn said.

Eddy looked at her watch. "Got to run, my plane is leaving soon. I have to get through security on time for my flight." She kissed Quinn on the cheek and trotted out of the restaurant.

"Crap! She left me with the bill." Quinn fumbled through her purse for her wallet.

Chapter Twenty-Three

Red, white, and blue bursts cracked the sky. Truck beds and lawn furniture filled with families and friends lined the parking lot of the Farmington mall.

"I can't believe I'm sitting on a tailgate watching such great fireworks," Quinn told Linda Lou between the thundering claps. "In Southern California, you'd have to pay to see something like this on the Fourth of July."

"Enjoy yourself." Linda Lou reached into the ice chest behind them, fished out a diet root beer, and handed it to her.

"Big city folks have lost the hometown spirit of the Fourth," Hugo said. "Everything is designed to make a buck. Watching free fireworks with the whole town has been a tradition around here for years." He shifted his weight on the lawn chair in the back of the truck.

"He's just pontificating like all good lawyers," Linda Lou said.

Quinn saw his chair sway to one side. *I wonder if it's going to collapse.* She shot a glance at Linda Lou.

"Don't worry, it's sturdier than it looks," she whispered. "And if it gives way, who's he going to sue—himself?"

"You're evil," Quinn murmured.

"Hey, Davis," Hugo bellowed at the pickup parked beside them. "Turn the radio up so we can hear the patriotic music better."

"Sure thing." Turning sideways he reached back by the wheel well and turned the volume up on Lee Greenwood's *God Bless the USA*.

"I love the way the music is coordinated with the fireworks," Linda Lou chirped.

Quinn studied Bunny and Davis snuggling on the rusty tailgate of their truck. "Those two look made for each other."

"I don't know why in the world I never figured out her mystery boyfriend was Davis. He was her first real crush in high school. But he never had eyes for anyone but Millie back then. He didn't pay much mind to Bunny," Linda Lou said.

"Well, looks like she's getting plenty of attention now."

Linda Lou looked over her shoulder at Hugo. She patted the space beside her. "Grab that pillow by the ice chest and come sit by me, honey."

Quinn sighed. *Will I ever call a man honey again?*

Hugo lumbered over and slipped in beside Linda Lou.

Two teenage boys wandered past the trucks staring at Quinn and her friends.

"Just a bunch of creps," the taller one said when they were not quite out of earshot. The other boy chortled and kept walking.

"Did he just call us creeps?" Linda Lou bristled.

"No, he called us *creps*. It's teen lingo for old people," Quinn said. "Maybe they'll come back and I can trip them with my de-*crep*-it foot." She grinned.

"Now, who's evil?" Linda Lou fluffed her hair. "We don't look that old, do we?"

"It's all a matter of perspective," Hugo said. "But you, my darling, look as fresh as a new morning." He kissed Linda Lou on the forehead.

"Davis, turn that music down. I want to hear all of Hugo's flattering," she yelled.

He tipped his cowboy hat and adjusted the volume.

Quinn felt like a fifth wheel with a gnawing emptiness in the pit of her stomach. "Got anymore of those double chocolate chip cookies?"

"Right behind you in the blue tin box," Linda Lou said.

Quinn pried the top off and wolfed down three giant cookies, but she did not feel any better.

"Have you heard from Megan since the wedding?" Linda Lou asked.

"She sent me a postcard of a volcano erupting last week," Quinn said between munches on her fourth cookie.

Linda Lou raised her brows and rolled her eyes.

"No, smarty-pants," Quinn said, "I don't think it was supposed to be symbolic. Anyway, she said she'd call after the Fourth."

"I've never been to Hawaii—just seen pictures."

"Patrick and I went to Kauai once. The Napali Coast was so lush. If I ever go back, I'm going to take one of those raft excursions along the shore and go snorkeling."

"Sounds wonderful. I'd sure like to go," Linda Lou mused.

"Maybe we should go this fall." Hugo lifted her hand and kissed it.

The marching beat of *Stars and Stripes Forever,* soared to a crescendo. Cymbals crashed and a final burst of fireworks bombarded the night. The music faded and the sky cleared.

Quinn grabbed two more cookies and jumped off the tailgate. "Well, guess I'd better get started home." She smiled but her eyes looked sad.

"You okay, sweetie?" Linda Lou asked.

"Yeah."

"See you at the fitness center Tuesday then?"

"Sure. Thanks for inviting me everybody." She waved and strolled to her Tahoe. Leaning against the door she finished off the cookies before climbing inside. Several minutes passed while she stifled a sob and stared at nothing through the driver's window.

Stop feeling sorry for yourself! She stuck the key in the ignition, turned on the vehicle, and started home.

Quinn increased the incline on the treadmill and ramped up the speed.

"Sorry I'm late." Linda Lou panted and hopped onto the machine next to Quinn's. "I haven't even had a chance to grab a bite to eat. Hugo and I had some last minute business to take care of at the office."

"Monkey business?" Quinn asked.

Linda Lou smirked.

"Anyway, you're not that late. But maybe you should catch your breath before you start working out."

"What? And lose my momentum. Not a chance. How many miles have you gone?"

"Two." Quinn kept her eyes focused forward.

"I can remember when you couldn't even finish a quarter mile without resting."

"Yeah. Well, times change. Ever since those two brats called us creps, I've been determined to work even harder."

"Onward and upward." Linda Lou raised her arm and clinched her fist. "What did Megan have to say when she called?"

"They had a wonderful time in Hawaii until Perry fell off a horse and broke his arm."

"Good heavens! How is he?"

"He'll be fine." Perspiration began to form on Quinn's forehead. She gripped the side rails so hard her knuckles turned white. "Then Megan announced that Mack Worthington, he's Perry's godfather, was excited when he found out where I live. He told her he'd always wanted to fish the quality waters of the San Juan."

"The place is famous among fly fisherman. People come from all over the world to fish here, you know."

"Yeah, yeah. Well, she invited him to stay with me because I live so close to the river."

"What?"

"She didn't even ask me, just up and invited him." Quinn ran faster. She wiped the sweat from her eyes with the back of her hand.

"Why would she do such a thing?"

"She said that since Mack let them stay at his ranch for their honeymoon, she thought it was only fair I let him stay in my spare bedroom while he's here."

"That was damn generous of her."

"I'll say."

"What's he like?"

"I don't know. I've never met him."

"No!" Linda Lou gasped. "I hope he's not one of those criminal types." She missed a step. "You can't be too careful with strangers nowadays." She struggled to regain her balance.

"Jeez, are you okay?" Quinn reached to help steady her friend. "I didn't mean to scare you. He was at the wedding reception. I didn't meet him but he's probably harmless."

"Are you sure? There are a lot of weirdoes out there, sweetie."

"From what I know, he seems respectable enough. He's well-heeled and old friend of Perry's family. And, after all, he is my son-in-law's godfather. I'm sure this visit was Megan's idea. She's decided I should meet this guy and once she's made up her mind there is no stopping her. She doesn't give a crap what I think."

"Hmm ... rich, daughter likes him. Maybe he's got potential. You know, it's time you found a man," Linda Lou puffed.

"Get serious. He's coming here to fish. It just irks me that she invited him without asking me first."

Linda Lou looked askance. "Would you have said yes?"

"I don't know."

"That's why she didn't ask you. When is he coming?"

"Next week."

"Wow, I was going to ask you to go out for some pie after we're done here, but you need to start dieting right now."

"Give me a break!"

Quinn stared at page one of her mystery novel for the fourth time.

Why can't I even get past the first paragraph?

She leaned back in the chaise lounge. Out of habit she reached for her bookmark to slip inside the novel but the small table next to the lounge was empty.

How could I have been so careless and lost it in Paris?

She set the book on her lap. Her gaze drifted to the river and upstream where she spied a man and a young child fishing. The child's line tightened and the man rushed to help land the fish.

Patrick and Rick loved to fish together. Why did you have to ruin everything, Patrick?

A year and three months had passed since his death. Her anger was gone, but a bottomless void remained. The same void she felt on the Fourth of July.

Green eyes peered out from behind a flowerpot in the corner of the deck.

"Where did you come from?"

A fluffy, white-faced, black cat padded to her side and looked up.

"Sure, I can use some company today," Quinn said to him. "So, what's your opinion about Patrick?"

The cat cocked his head to one side and twitched an ear.

"Do you think I would have forgiven him, if I'd known what was going on?"

Meow. The cat tilted his head the other direction.

"I don't think so either. How could've I ever forgiven him? Our marriage would have been over." Quinn moved the book to the table next the lounge. She crossed her arms and looked into the cat's face. "Now, how about Sam Maxwell?"

Lifting a front paw the cat began lapping at his pads.

Quinn laughed. "Licking my wounds, huh? I don't think you're too far off the mark." She stood, bowed low in front of the cat and placed her right palm on her forehead. "Salaam, wise one. Tell me how I can get rid of the emptiness in my heart."

The cat looked up at her.

"No answer?"

The black and white mass of fur looked over his shoulder toward the north. Stretching across the distant horizon was a brilliant rainbow.

"That's a sign of a new beginning," she told the cat. "It's the promise of something good ahead." Sunlight glinted off a speck of gold buried in the fur beneath his neck. "What's that? An identification tag?"

The cat mewed and rubbed against Quinn's leg.

She picked up the little creature and pushed the black fluff away from the tag. "Let me take a look and see who you belong to." One word was engraved in large letters.

"MAX."

A chill rand down her spine—she almost dropped the cat.

Chapter Twenty-Four

There was not a speck of dust in the spare bedroom after Quinn completed her morning cleaning. She placed a stack of fresh blue towels on the corner of the dresser and fluffed the pillows on the newly made bed. On the nightstand, she set a copy of Tony Hillerman's *Skinwalkers* from Uncle Sean's library.

She trudged back into the living room, collapsed on the sofa, and closed her eyes intending to rest for a few minutes. Two hours passed before she opened them again.

Sitting upright, she stared at the clock above the television. "Jeez, he'll be here in an hour."

She scurried into the bathroom and groaned at her image in the mirror—no makeup, disheveled hair, and dirty clothes. She scrubbed her face and snatched her cosmetic bag from under the vanity. On went foundation, eyebrow pencil, and blush.

"I need to get rid of half of this stuff," she said, searching through the bulging bag for her eyeliner.

She dumped the contents of the bag into the sink. An eye shadow case shattered against the marble basin, releasing a blue powdery mist that settled over everything in the washbowl.

"Crap!" She kicked the vanity. With a handful of tissue, she wiped the blue coating off her eyeliner and candy pink lipstick. After feathering the liner into her eyelashes, she put on lipstick and tossed all of the cosmetics back into the bag. In one swoop, she pulled off her T-shirt and used it to wipe the blue powder out of the sink. She threw the soiled shirt on the floor and stuffed the cosmetic bag back under the sink.

Picking at her hair, she attempted to add volume and straighten out the tangles. "This is impossible," she whined. "Oh, why should I care what he thinks anyway?"

She picked up the dirty T-shirt, scampered across the hall, and tossed it into the hamper in her bedroom. Quickly, she changed into the new pair of jeans and pink blouse she had set out earlier.

Quinn checked her watch. "I've still got twenty minutes left." She sighed, sauntered back out to the kitchen, and guzzled a can of diet root beer from the fridge. Eyeing the bulletin board, she threw a kiss at the hunk on Eddy's postcard.

The sun shone warm against her back through the kitchen window. She turned to admire the flowers blooming in the courtyard. Instead, her eyes locked on the sink beneath the window.

"I forgot the dishes!" A hot flash gripped her and she jumped into overdrive—washing the dishes and wiping down the counter. By the time the last drop of water swirled down the drain, her body temperature had returned to near normal.

She peeked at the front of her shirt. *Thank goodness, no water spots.*

Clang. Clang.

"The cowbell—I didn't hear anyone drive up. He can't be here already," she said, scanning the courtyard.

A tall, lanky man dressed in tan slacks and a maroon polo shirt plodded toward the door. He struggled to balance a suitcase, an armful of fishing equipment, and a laptop computer. His face was obscured by a fishing hat pulled low on his forehead and a pair of aviator sunglasses perched on his nose.

The doorbell rang. Quinn finished the last swig of root beer and headed toward the entryway. She took a deep breath, rubbed her hands on the sides of her new jeans, and opened the door.

"Hi, I'm Mack," the man said, setting down his belongings and removing his sunglasses.

"Sam … Sam Maxwell?" she said, barely audible. Blood drained from her face—she could hardly breathe.

"Maxwell Samuel Worthington, ma'am." He grinned, revealing his perfect white teeth. "I'm sometimes known as Sam Maxwell, but my friends just call me Mack. You must be Quinn, thanks for inviting me. I've wanted to fish the quality water of the San Juan for a long time."

"Um … um …" Her knees felt unsteady. She pressed the palm of her left hand against the wall for support. Her heart palpitated. *Ba-boom, ba-boom, ba-boom.*

"Is it okay if I come in?" he asked.

She drew in a breath. *I'm not sure I can talk without my tongue hanging out the side of my mouth.*

"Oh, I'm sorry," she stammered. "Of course, please come right in … ah … the guest room is right down the hall. Ah … on your right."

"Right, on the right." He gave her a wink and walked across the living room toward the hall.

"He must think I'm a moron," she muttered under her breath, and followed him into the bedroom. "If you need anything, just let me know. Would you like a soda or a beer?"

"Thanks, but I'm fine." He pulled back the window curtain and studied the sky. "Looks like I might be able to get in a couple hours of fishing before dark. What do you think?"

"Probably." She leaned against the doorjamb trying to look nonchalant while her heart hammered. *Ba-boom, ba-boom.* "Do you like spaghetti?" *Ba-boom.* "I thought I'd fix some for dinner." *Ba-boom.*

"Sure, sounds great." He turned away from the window and removed his hat revealing his silver hair.

She rubbed the sides of her jeans before blurting, "Megan said your hair was red and you wore glasses."

"The hair was for a movie I was making, and I'd lost one of my contacts." He smiled. "Say, you wouldn't know how to get to the Texas Hole, would you?"

"I haven't the foggiest." *Ba-boom.* "I don't fish."

"Too bad," he said with a sly smile. "We could have fun."

For an instant she thought he was flirting with her. "I'm sure they can point you in the right direction at Abe's." *Ba-boom.*

"Where's that?"

"You can't miss it. It's on the main road leading toward the dam."

Fifteen minutes later, he grabbed his fishing gear and was on his way.

Quinn sat on the sofa wondering if she was dreaming again. She rose and hurried into the kitchen. Grabbing the phone, she punched in Eddy's number. The phone rang five times.

Maybe she's not home.

Two more rings.

"Hello."

"It's me," Quinn said. "I ..."

"Omigod!" Eddy cut her off. "I just had lunch with Marty, and boy, have I got news for you." She took a quick breath. "You're not going to believe this—Sam Maxwell and Mack Worthington are the same guy!"

"I know ... I ..."

Eddy cut her off again. "That's why Marty was at the wedding, he's Sam's—I mean Mack's manager. Did you just say you know?"

"Yes. Not about Marty, but I know Sam and Mack are the same person." Quinn's hand started to tremble.

"You know? How do you know?"

"He's here. Sam is here." She tightened her grip on the receiver to stop the shaking.

"You've got to be kidding me."

"Megan invited him. He's here to go fishing. In fact, that's what he's doing right now—fishing."

"This is a joke, right?"

"No. He really is here. What should I do?"

"Go for it girl. This may be your only chance. I can't believe we chased him halfway around the world and then, just like that, he drops in for a visit. You go for it."

Quinn gulped. "Okay." *Ba-boom.*

Déjà vu. Quinn stood in the kitchen dressed in the same outfit she had planned to wear for Patrick's postmortem celebration—the same sheer garnet blouse with matching pushup bra, the same tight jeans, high-heeled garnet sandals, chandelier earrings, and the same teardrop diamond pendant resting above her cleavage.

Maybe this is a bit over the top, she said to herself, and studied her reflection in the kitchen window. *The earrings do look a little slutty with the rest of this outfit.* She took them off and placed them in a coffee cup on the counter. *Last time I dressed like this, all I wanted was revenge. Now, I just want a second look from Mack. I won't chicken out, and I won't babble like a fool again.*

Everything was ready for when Mack's returned from fishing. A vase of cut flowers from the courtyard decorated the dining room table and the silverware and plates were set out. She had prepared a lettuce and tomato salad with mushrooms sprinkled on top and popped it into the fridge. The sauce simmered on the stove and the water for the spaghetti noodles boiled. Garlic bread wrapped in aluminum foil sat on the counter next to the oven.

Ever since her Paris fantasy, Quinn kept a bottle of cabernet sauvignon on hand. She placed the bottle on the counter and mused over the irony of the situation.

A car turned onto her gravel driveway.

It has to be him. I can do this. I can do this. She opened the front door.

"Hi," he said, waving as he strode through the gate. He stopped next to the ceramic fountain and removed his waders. "Is there a place out here to hang these?"

Even in his long johns, with bare feet and dirt smeared across his face, he made Quinn's heart jump. "There's a hook on the wall near the gate. I think that's what it's for."

His shirttail swayed as he walked across the courtyard and she caught a glimpse of his tight buns.

Whew!

He hung up the waders and returned to the house. "By the way, you look smashing," he said, stepping past her and heading down the hall. "Nice necklace."

Ba-boom.

"Dinner is ready whenever you are," she called after him.

"I'll just take a quick shower and be there in a few minutes."

She pictured his body as she remembered it in *Inspired by a Kiss*. The thought of steamy water running off his muscled chest and down his abs sent a tingle to her toes.

In the kitchen, she put the noodles into the water and the garlic bread in the oven. She resisted an urge to take a swig of wine.

Ten minutes later, Mack peeked into the kitchen. "Can I help?"

"You can take the salad out of the fridge and put it on the table. I'll have the rest ready in a jiffy."

Neither spoke as they filled their plates. Quinn noticed that the Hillerman novel from the guestroom now sat on the edge of the table near Mack. A golden tassel dangled from its pages.

He hasn't had time to read yet, has he?

Mack chomped down on a bite of salad. "What's this dressing?"

"Raspberry walnut, it's one of my favorites."

"It's very good." He picked up the book.

Quinn lifted a fork of spaghetti into her mouth.

He pulled the bookmark out of the novel. "Marty, my manager, found this in the hotel lobby on his last trip to Paris."

Quinn's mouth dropped open and sauce dribbled down her chin when she saw the hand-tooled, leather marker. She snatched the napkin from her lap and dabbed her face.

"He said he picked it up because of the *M* on it. But since he doesn't read many books he decided to give it to me." Mack held the marker in one hand and nervously rubbed the tassel between the fingers of his other. "Megan saw me using it at the ranch and said it was just like one of yours. She said you'd recently been to Paris, and thought maybe you lost it on your trip."

"It belonged to my grandfather. I didn't think I'd ever see it again."

"Here, it's yours then," he said taking her hand and placing the marker in her palm. "I'm glad I could get it back to you." He squeezed her hand closed.

Ba-boom!

"Did you enjoy your trip?" he asked.

Ba-boom. "What?"

"Did you enjoy your trip to Paris?"

"Oh, yes," she said refocusing. "A friend took me for my birthday. We had a great time."

"It's one of my favorite cities, especially at night," he said.

They continued eating in silence. Quinn concentrated on not spilling any more food.

"The meal was delicious," he said, after sopping up the last of his spaghetti sauce with a slice of garlic bread. "If you don't mind, I'm going to turn in early. It's been a long day." He stood and headed for his bedroom before Quinn could respond.

She cleared the dishes and cleaned up the kitchen.

Later, on her way down the hall she noticed he left the wet towels from his shower on the floor of the bathroom.

Jeez, I guess all men are alike. Even neatnik Patrick left his towels on the floor. Or, maybe Mack was just in a hurry to see me again—fat chance.

She picked up the damp heap of towels and took it to the laundry room. Before going to bed, she placed fresh towels in the bathroom.

Quinn stared at the ceiling, rolled onto her stomach, bunched up her pillow, and turned onto her side. She pulled up the covers, kicked off the covers, and got tangled in the covers. The whole routine repeated itself for the next three hours.

She thought she heard Mack in the bathroom but decided she was imagining things. It was unsettling to have him sleeping so close. Over and over again, she pondered why he never checked out her cleavage during dinner. She had tried so hard to look sexy.

Maybe the little squeeze he gave my hand meant something. Oh, who am I kidding?

Around two in the morning, nature called and she staggered into the dark bathroom. She pulled up her nightgown, backed up to the commode and sat down.

"Crap!" Her bottom hit the cold rim of the ceramic toilet and she sank into an awkward position. "Give me a break, not another man who can't remember to put the seat down."

Chapter Twenty-Five

A knock on her bedroom door awakened Quinn. She grumbled, rolled onto her stomach, and glanced at the clock—six AM. "What?" she moaned.

"I just wanted to tell you not to fix supper. I thought I'd grill fish tonight."

She jolted upright remembering who was on the other side of the door.

Ba-boom!

"Th ... Thanks," she stammered. "What about breakfast? Give me a minute and I'll fix you something."

"Don't worry. I picked up some stuff at Abe's yesterday. I'm fine," Mack said. "See you around five. Remember, don't fix anything."

"Okay." She wondered what he was going to do if he didn't catch any fish.

A few minutes later she heard the front door close. She dragged herself out of bed and wandered into the kitchen. After eating breakfast, she took a shower, washed a load of clothes, and spent the rest of the morning reading a book.

Megan called around noon. "Well, what do you think of him, Mom?"

"Who?" Quinn paused for emphasis. "Oh, you mean Sam Maxwell—the movie star."

"Sam who?" Megan said playfully.

"Don't lie to me young lady. Why didn't you tell me it was him?"

"Sorry, Mom. Honest, I didn't know he was an actor until I saw some movie posters at his ranch."

"Well, you could've given me a heads-up once you knew."

"I thought it would be a great surprise."

"Oh, I was a surprised all right. I almost fell over."

"How are the two of you getting along?" Megan asked.

"Okay, I guess. He returned grandpa's bookmark. He's fishing right now. I sure hope he catches something because he said was going to grill fish tonight."

"I thought you told me the quality waters of the San Juan were 'catch and release' only. Where is he getting the fish?"

Quinn thought for a moment. "Danged if I know."

"I wonder what he's up to." Megan said. "Anyway, keep me in the loop. I know you two will hit it off."

After Megan hung up, Quinn strolled out to the courtyard. She sat in one of the carved chairs and propped her feet on the edge of her favorite terra cotta pot. Her body relaxed and her eyes closed. The image of the tapestry in her Paris hotel room came into focus. She zeroed in on the Patrick-like devil in its corner and smiled.

You'll never make me feel inferior again, Patrick.

There was no anger, no bitterness left in her thoughts. It was not that she had forgiven him—she probably never would. But his betrayal no longer held her prisoner.

I'm okay, she said to herself.

A gentle purr, like the engine of a small airplane, stirred her from her thoughts. She opened her eyes just as Max bounded over the wall into the courtyard.

"Oh, so it's you again. I can use some company."

Max sprung onto her lap and nestled his neck in the crook of her right arm. She stroked his head.

"Guess who else is visiting me? His name is Max, too. Well, technically it's Maxwell."

Purr ... purr ... purr.

"And just like you, he's a nice guy." *Who am I kidding—a cat? Mack is more than a nice guy, he's downright charming—not perfect, but definitely intriguing.*

Purr ... purr ... purr.

"Too bad, Max, I don't think he's interested in me." She ruffled his ears. "But you like me, don't you?"

The fur ball snuggled closer.

"Besides he's just been a fantasy of mine, a coping mechanism to deal with the whole Patrick mess. I hardly know him."

Just before five Mack came through the gate dressed in dark gray slacks and a heather gray polo shirt. He carried a grocery bag in each arm.

Quinn opened the front door and caught a whiff of his cologne as he entered.

Jeez, he smells good. "I thought you were going fishing. Where are your waders?" she asked, leaning toward him for another whiff.

"In the car with the rest of my gear. I changed in the parking lot before I went into town to get the salmon."

She looked puzzled.

"Oh," he laughed, "you didn't think I was going to cook *illegal* trout, did you?"

"Well ..."

He cocked his head to one side. "I'm a law-abiding citizen. Now, go watch television or something while I fix supper."

"Can I help?"

"Nope. This is man's work tonight. Stay out of my way."

She walked across the living room and sat in the corner of the couch. She reached for the novel on the coffee table and tried to read but could not concentrate.

Mack rumbled around in the kitchen. Quinn heard the clinking of pots and pans.

"Need any help finding things?" she called.

"It's under control," he replied.

A half hour later, he set the meal on the table and called, "Dinner's ready." Quinn took a seat as he poured iced tea into their glasses.

"This is great," she said, tasting the salmon with mango salsa.

"Thanks, I'd hoped you'd like my concoction."

"Did you catch any fish today?" she asked, trying to make small talk.

"A couple of little rainbow trout."

Rainbow—there's that word again. She nervously rubbed one hand on the side of her jeans.

"The big ones weren't biting today."

"Too bad." She inhaled to steady herself and went back to eating the steamed green beans."

After Mack finished eating he said, "I have a confession to make. I had an ulterior motive for coming here."

Quinn thought he looked uneasy.

"When Megan told me about the bookmark, she showed me your picture in her wallet. I recognized you as the woman who fell into the water trough on the set of *Turquoise Trail.* That was you, wasn't it?"

She swallowed her last bite of salmon. "Yes," she said, shifting in her chair.

"I tried to find you that day, to see if you were okay." He paused as though not sure he should continue. "Because ... when I saw you through the window something about you fascinated me."

Did he really say that? She could barely breathe.

He smiled sheepishly. "Of course, that was before your mouth dropped open and you fell into the water."

She relaxed.

"Still, I'm sure it was your eyes that got to me. They're beautiful, you know."

"Um …" she began.

"Time to do dishes," he said cutting her off. He picked up their plates and carried them into the kitchen.

Her hands shook as she followed him with the empty glasses.

Is now the time to tell him I've been thinking about him too? She set the glasses next to the sink. *No, not yet.*

Mack put the plates on the counter and turned toward her. "I thought I saw you in Los Angeles—caught in the middle of the sprinklers near our movie set. But you were gone in a flash."

"Yep, that was me, drenched again." She forced a smile.

Mack chuckled and his eyes sparkled.

Ba-boom!

Quinn rubbed her hands on the sides of her jeans. "I'll wash," she said, taking the detergent out of the cabinet and filling the sink with water.

Mack picked up the dishtowel. "I'm an expert drier. It was my job when I was a kid."

"Mine too," she said. "Mom didn't get a dish washer until I was in high school."

Their casual discussion continued until after the dishes were put away.

"When Megan told me you lived by the San Juan River, I knew it was my chance to meet you. So, I finagled an invitation to come out here."

Quinn leaned against the counter and faced him. *Now is the time.* "When I went to Paris, I knew you were filming there and I was hoping I'd get a chance to see you. Oh, it was my birthday, but what I really wanted was to meet you."

He grinned and stepped closer to her.

She blushed. "And, that's what I was doing in LA, too."

Mack touched the side of her neck with the back of his hand and kissed her forehead. "Destiny has a way of playing tricks," he said.

"It sure does." She couldn't move.

There was an uncomfortable hush.

"Do you have a Scrabble game around here?" he asked, his eyes searching the room.

"Oh, I love to play. I'll get it." She rushed into the living room and returned with the game.

"I taught Perry to play when he was seven," Mack said.

"Oh, no." She frowned. "He's trounced me every time we've played, and now you'll probably beat me too."

Mack smiled. "Don't worry. He's been beating me regularly since he was fifteen."

For the next two days, Mack fished and Quinn followed her usual routine. They took turns cooking dinner and played Scrabble in the evenings. Their talk flowed as easily as it had in Quinn's Paris fantasy.

On Tuesday Quinn went to the fitness center and out to lunch with Linda Lou.

"How's your houseguest?" Linda Lou cackled, between bites her chef's salad. "He hasn't shown any signs of being a weirdo yet, has he?"

"Quite the opposite."

"Tell me the truth—you know I'm only looking out for you, sweetie. What's he really like?"

"He's very nice." Quinn poked at her chicken salad. "He's a good Scrabble player, and …"

"No, what does he *look* like?" Linda Lou raised her eyebrows.

"Oh, he's tall, has gray hair, nice teeth—just a regular guy." *There's no way in hell I'm telling her who he really is or it will be all over town in no time.*

"A regular, *rich* guy."

"Yep," Quinn said.

"Well, like I said before, you'd better give him a look-see. He could be the one for you."

"You never know."

Chapter Twenty-Six

Mack returned from fishing late that afternoon and disappeared down the hall to clean up. A short time later, he ambled into the living room carrying a picture frame with a broken glass.

"I'm sorry, it fell off the closet shelf when I was putting up some of my gear," he told Quinn. "I'll be glad to replace the frame. It doesn't look like the photo is damaged."

"Don't worry about it," she said and leaned back in the corner of the couch. "I wasn't planning on hanging it back up."

Mack studied the photo for a moment. "I think I know the guy on the right." He showed the photo to Quinn.

Her eyes widened.

"Yes, I'm sure of it," he said. "I played poker with him in Las Vegas a while back. He had a pretty long-legged girlfriend with him named Kathy. That's why I remember him, she was a knockout. I think his name was Pat."

"No, his name was Rat!" She grabbed the picture out of his hand. "He's my dead husband. I didn't know about his affair with her until after they were both dead."

"Both dead?"

"They were killed together in a car accident. I found out later that they'd been carrying on for a long time."

Mack sat down beside her. "Does Megan know?"

"She and Rick know that the circumstances of their dad's death were, to say the least, awkward. They came up with a lot of explanations for Patrick and Kathy being together. I'm sure they couldn't face the truth. I didn't tell them everything I found out—I didn't want to sully their memories of their father. They probably would have thought I was just being vindictive anyway."

"You're a better woman than the ones I know." He put his arm around her shoulder. "After our divorce, my ex-wife trashed me with everyone we knew and anyone else who would listen. It still makes me angry when I think about her."

"I was really mad for a whole year after Patrick died, but I'm doing better now." She looked at the photo again and then placed it upside down on the coffee table.

"I think you need some cheering up," Mack said. "How about we go fishing tomorrow?"

"Fishing? I've never ..."

"Well, it's about time you did." He stood up and reached for her hand.

"I don't know, it's not really my thing," she said as he pulled her to her feet.

"How do you know if you've never tried it? Listen, I have to leave the day after tomorrow, so there's no time for arguing. Let's go into town and buy you some gear and we can get something to eat while we're at it."

"My uncle left a storage room full of fishing stuff," she said. "He wasn't much taller than me, so I'm sure we can find anything I need in there." She got up from the couch and led him to the room.

"Wow. It's like an Orvis store in here," he said, peeking inside.

"Told you." Quinn stepped into the room. "Still, if you're not worried someone will recognize you, I'd enjoy eating in town."

"People usually don't recognize me." He followed her inside and pulled a wide-brimmed fishing hat off a hook near the door. "The most people usually say is that I remind them of someone.

But, I'll wear this just in case," he said, placing the hat on his head. "We can get you a fishing license while we're in town."

The next morning Mack and Quinn decked out in their neoprene waders, fishing vests, and wide-brimmed hats drove toward the Texas Hole.

"How much farther is it?" she asked.

"We'll turn at the church. See it there on top of that small hill on the left." He pointed to a little tan chapel. "Then it's just a short drive to the quality waters."

"It's strange to see a church out here all by itself," Quinn said.

"It reminds me to be thankful for this beautiful area." Mack turned onto the road winding past the church.

A short distance from the river they pulled into an almost empty lot. They parked a few feet away from a picnic table. Nearby a stocky man in long johns stood next to a truck putting on his chest waders.

"Does everyone get dressed in the parking lot?" Quinn asked remembering Mack said he had changed there.

"Not everyone, but I saw a woman in her bikini underwear here yesterday. Come on, let's get our gear and head for the river," he said, handing her a pair of sunglasses attached to a lanyard.

Mack led the way to a trail veering off to the left of the lot. The path was strewn with smooth river rocks, tall grasses and thickets. Quinn almost stumbled several times on the uneven terrain.

"I'm glad you made me wear this long sleeved shirt," she called and swatted at the switches blocking her way.

"You can never be too prepared." Mack carried their fly rods and a small ice chest. He trod up the path at a steady pace stopping now and then for Quinn to catch up.

At the river's edge, trampled reeds and mud formed small berms. They walked the narrow footpath along the side of the river for a short distance.

"This looks like a good spot," he said and set down their gear.

Near the shore the water appeared green with moss-covered river rocks and silt lining the river bottom.

"Yuck," Quinn said and looked upriver. Whitecaps formed as the water tumbled down a small rocky decline. A man in full fishing regalia cast his line just below the whitecaps. She looked downriver. A young woman in flip-flops, capris, and striped T-shirt fished from a large rock in shallow water.

Guess you don't need all this fancy equipment to catch fish.

"Let's give it a try?" Mack said and helped her into the river. "Watch where you step the mossy stones are really slippery."

They waded out to about knee depth and Mack showed her how to cast her line.

"Remember, you are casting the line upstream, don't worry about the fly. Now, let the line drift back past you. That's right, you've got it."

After a half hour of practice, he announced, "You're on your own."

"Wait! Don't leave me," she called as he headed downriver. "Where are you going?"

"We shouldn't stand too close together or our lines might get tangled. Signal me if you catch anything," he said and continued a few more yards before stopping.

Quinn stayed in her area and followed Mack's instructions—oblivious to the passage of time. The drifting of her line, the pressure of the water against her body, the smell of the stream gave her a sense of oneness with the river—something she had never felt from her back deck.

Maybe I should have tried this with Patrick when he asked.

The sun was high in the sky when Mack waded toward her.

"It must be close to lunchtime. Want to stop and eat our sandwiches?" he asked.

"I didn't realize standing in a river could make me so hungry. I'm starving." She turned and started toward the shore.

"It's the flow of the water that wears you out," he said.

A Canada goose by the opposite bank squawked angrily. An equally harsh squall answered. Wings beat as the giant birds screeched in rage. They skated across the river in a wild chase. Quinn ducked as they came near and tried to scurry out of their way but her boots slipped on the rocks.

Mack rushed toward her. He grabbed for her arm but missed. Thrown off balance, they both ended up on their butts in waist deep water.

"Saved by our chest waders," Quinn laughed.

"You know what they say—water is a sign of rebirth," he said.

"Well, I certainly must be close to being reborn after all the dunking I've taken this year." She struggled to stand.

He boosted himself to his feet, took her hand, and grinned. "Maybe this year will be a new beginning for both of us."

Ba-boom!

Together they trudged to the shore and sat on the bank.

"Are you okay?" he asked

"I'm fine. How about you?"

"Nothing a kiss won't cure," he answered. "How about it?"

She tilted her head and smiled.

His soft kiss turned into a passionate embrace.

Ba-boom! Ba-boom!

"Wow!" he said as their lips parted.

Quinn sighed and leaned back under a small tree. "Kiss me again."

An hour later Mack asked "Now, where are those sandwiches?"

That evening after dinner they walked onto the back deck and stood by the railing. The reflection of the mauve sunset danced on the surface of the flowing water.

"I always feel calm out here." Quinn said as a blue heron glided to a landing on the opposite bank. "Before you leave, I want you to know you're always welcome here."

He put his arm around her waist and pulled her close. "Next month when you come to California to sell your house you're staying with me."

"Okay, but first you have to promise to help me get rid of Patrick's chair."

"It's a done deal." His lips tenderly touched her ear. "You know you take my breath away, don't you?" he murmured.

"Do I?"

His warm mouth brushed her cheek and caressed her lips. *Ba-boom! Ba-boom! Ba-boom!*

Acknowledgements

Special thanks to Lee Pierce for lending his expertise to help edit the final draft and to Judy Castleberry for her insightful observations regarding the continuity of the manuscript. Additional thanks to Roberta Summers, Floyd Pearce, Connie Gotsch, my husband Bob and my daughter Robin Bellah—their comments and suggestions improved the story and my writing.

CPSIA information can be obtained
at www.ICGtesting.com
Printed in the USA
FFOW02n0401250417
34934FF

9 781440 193958